Was he saying what she thought he was saying?

Was the gorgeous, emotionally unavailable, confirmed bachelor, billionaire Adam Tyler saying that he would like them to try each other on for size?

Adam watched her with his usual quiet patience. Well, he would have to wait. Her answer would be one of the most important of her life.

Think, Cara. Think!

Gorgeous—God, yes.

Emotionally unavailable—surely as much as ever. But aren't you the same?

Confirmed bachelor—meaning he would never try to change you so as to keep you. Isn't that perfect?

Billionaire.

That was where it all fell apart.

D0018551

ALLY BLAKE

worked in retail, danced on television and acted in friends' short films until the writing bug could no longer be ignored. And as her mother had read romance novels ever since Ally was a baby, the aspiration to write novels had almost been bred into her. Ally married her gorgeous husband, Mark, in Las Vegas (no Elvis in sight, thank you very much), and they live in beautiful Melbourne, Australia. Her husband cooks, he cleans and he's the love of her life. How's that for a hero?

Next month escape to Italy, with some of the characters you know and love from this story in

A Mother for His Daughter (#1845)
in Silhouette Romance®

For a heartwarming read, set in the jewel of Australia's crown—the Great Barrier Reef—don't miss another of Ally Blake's exciting new novels

Meant-To-Be Mother (#3930)
On sale in January 2007
only from Harlequin Romance®!

How to
Marry
a
Billionaire

ALLY BLAKE

SILHOUETTE *Romance* ®

Published by Silhouette Books

America's Publisher of Contemporary Romance

If you purchased this book without a cover you should be aware
that this book is stolen property. It was reported as "unsold and
destroyed" to the publisher, and neither the author nor the
publisher has received any payment for this "stripped book."

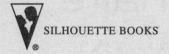 SILHOUETTE BOOKS

ISBN-13: 978-0-373-19841-2
ISBN-10:   0-373-19841-8

HOW TO MARRY A BILLIONAIRE

Copyright © 2004 by Ally Blake

First North American Publication 2006

All rights reserved. Except for use in any review, the reproduction
or utilization of this work in whole or in part in any form by any
electronic, mechanical or other means, now known or hereafter
invented, including xerography, photocopying and recording, or in
any information storage or retrieval system, is forbidden without
the written permission of the editorial office, Silhouette Books,
233 Broadway, New York, NY 10279 U.S.A.

All characters in this book have no existence outside the imagination of
the author and have no relation whatsoever to anyone bearing the same
name or names. They are not even distantly inspired by any individual
known or unknown to the author, and all incidents are pure invention.

This edition published by arrangement with Harlequin Books S.A.

® and TM are trademarks of Harlequin Books S.A., used under license.
Trademarks indicated with ® are registered in the United States Patent
and Trademark Office, the Canadian Trade Marks Office and in other
countries.

Visit Silhouette Books at www.eHarlequin.com

Printed in U.S.A.

To one grandmother for the treasure troves
of romance novels that were always to
be found under her spare bed, and to the other
for coloring my life with *Dr. Seuss's ABC*.

CHAPTER ONE

IT WAS love at first sight.

'I have never seen anything more beautiful,' Cara said as she stared through the window of the stylish Chapel Street shoe store.

'You simply have to have them,' Gracie agreed, her nose pressed up against the window-pane.

'They're frivolous. Certainly not a necessity.'

'So be frivolous, while you're still young enough for it to be charming.'

'But they're Kate Madden Designs!' Cara pointed out, hoping that at least would be argument enough to stop her from making such a rash purchase.

'So?'

'So, they cost more than my father used to earn in a week!'

Gracie turned to her. 'Now that's the strangest reason I have ever heard for not spending one's own hard-earned money. Even from Cara, the Queen of Thrift.'

Cara decided it was best to keep focussing on the shoes.

'And how much do *you* earn a week?' Gracie asked as though talking to a two-year-old.

'More than my father,' Cara admitted.

'So there you go!' Gracie grabbed Cara by the upper arms and turned her so they were face to face, the shoes glistening on the periphery of their vision. 'You have no choice. This is the big time. This is *not* mucking about with styling mousse and safety pins in converted warehouses, styling emaciated models for magazines. This is *not* getting

7

kudos for finding designer clothes at bargain-basement prices. This is gold credit cards. This is limousines. This is television!' Gracie spread her hands before her as though indicating the way of the future. 'You want to make an impression and these are the shoes that will do it.'

Cara's gaze was irresistibly drawn back to the stunning creations sitting atop their own black velvet stand. The shoes were elegant, they were red, they were embroidered satin, and they had heels one could use as a lethal weapon if ever one found the need. In a word, they were unforgettable.

'And just think,' Gracie said, leaning her head on Cara's shoulder as she returned to her vigil before the coolest shoes ever made, 'if you don't get the job, at least you'll have a killer pair of shoes to console you.'

Cara nodded. The thing was, she had to get the job. She would be twenty-seven in a couple of months, the same age her father was the first time he filed for bankruptcy, and if her serious plans to have the St Kilda Storeys apartment building paid off by that time were to come to fruition, bar winning the Lotto, this was the only way it would be done.

And it *would* be done. There were no two ways about it. The property would be hers. Every brick. Every roof tile. Every grain of dirt. Only then would she be free of the constant feeling that one of those bricks resided in her chest.

Gracie was right. The fact that Cara was infamous for scouting out vintage pieces at charity shop prices would not hold her in much stead in the new crowd in which she would be moving. Television was about being cutting edge, not thrifty. And if she was going to land the high-paying job styling the star of the biggest television show ever to hit Australian screens, she would have to be unforgettable or bust.

*   *   *

'You have to be kidding me!' Adam said, his voice a mix of shock and laughter.

'Nope,' Chris returned with a big sunny grin. 'I'm going to be on TV as the main attraction in my very own dating programme.'

Adam's laughter dried up the moment he realised this was no laughing matter. Though his friend and business partner was practically a genius when it came to creating cutting-edge telecommunications innovations, he was not a practical joker.

'The contract was signed, sealed and delivered as of this morning,' Chris said.

Adam shot from his chair and paced up and down the room. 'I wish you had told me you were considering doing this, Chris. You really should have consulted me first.'

'Ah, no, I shouldn't have.'

Adam stopped pacing and glared at his friend. But Chris, who usually gave in to Adam's will, stared right back. This would take some care. 'You're the one who put me in charge of the public face of this company, and, as such, if you plan on doing anything that might alter Revolution Wireless's image in any way, you must consult me first.'

'This is not about the company,' Chris said. 'This is about me. Thus it is officially none of your business as Head of Marketing for Revolution Wireless. But as my friend, I wanted you to know.'

'Fine. Now, as your *friend*, I'm telling you it is the most ridiculous thing I have ever heard. A television dating show? Come on! If you're looking for a girl, I'll take you out and find you one. I know plenty of women who would be happy to escort one of Australia's most eligible bachelors.'

When Chris didn't budge, Adam grabbed him by the arm

and made to tug him out the door. 'There's literally millions of them out there in the real world. I can find you one on any street corner right now!'

Chris shrugged out of Adam's grasp, his fists clenched at his side. 'I don't want some escort girl I can pick up on any old street corner.'

Seeing how upset Chris was becoming, Adam took a moment to rein in his concern, which was fast running out of control. 'That's not what I meant and you know it.'

'I want a woman with whom to spend my quiet moments,' Chris explained. 'I want a wife. I certainly don't want one of your cast-offs. The women you date are the complete antithesis of what any sane man would want in a wife. Any man apart from your father, of course. While we're talking about relationships, let's talk about yours.'

Adam decided to ignore that final jab and focussed on the bits *he* wanted to focus on. 'This is about you, mate, not me, and my point is you could have anyone you want. Where has this all come from all of a sudden? Why now?'

Chris shrugged and softened a very little, his palms flattening out until they hung straight by his side. 'It's time. I work too much to go the regular route of dating by numbers. The years have slipped away without my even knowing it. I'm turning thirty-five this year.'

'I'm thirty-five already.'

That earned Adam two raised eyebrows.

'Chris, by the way you're acting anyone would think that was middle-aged. We're still young men, with our whole lives in front of us.'

'Exactly my point. While I am still a young man, I want someone with whom to share as much of that remaining time as possible.'

Adam felt himself running out of arguments and it bothered him to see Chris so certain. Sunny, cheery Chris, always glued to his laptop, creating brilliant business solutions for their hip, rising-star telecommunications company, was suddenly searching beyond the limits of his clever mind for satisfaction. The world outside had finally beckoned.

And despite his protestations about the effects Chris's plans would have on the image of the company, that wasn't really what had Adam spooked. He was perfectly aware that the big bad world could swallow a good-natured guy like Chris whole.

'OK, then,' Adam said, rallying his forces, focussing every lick of attention on his foolish friend, 'please explain to me why you think you need to go on a TV dating show to find a wife?'

'Because it's the only way I can meet women who have no idea who I am.'

Adam shook his head. 'Run that by me again.'

'The producers have gone to incredible trouble to pick out thirty women from all over Australia. Thirty attractive, accomplished, interesting women who have been given extensive compatibility tests. Thirty women who have no clue who owns Revolution Wireless, and thus have no idea how much I am worth. They will get to know me just for me. Chris, everyday Aussie bloke. Not Chris Geyer, richest single Australian man under forty.'

And *that* Adam understood. As two of the young owners of the Revolution Wireless telecommunications giant, one of Australia's fastest expanding business empires, he and Chris were considered prime pickings by the women in their regular social circles who knew *exactly* what they were worth.

Chris's earlier comments slammed into his thoughts. So what if he dated women dripping in diamonds and lofty aspirations, just like the ones who had taken his father to the cleaners over and over again? That way at least he had no chance of ever mistaking his feelings for any of them and therefore would never succumb to the same fate. And he had no intention of allowing his kind-hearted, naive friend to fall into that trap either. Especially with some buck-toothed ignoramus chosen by a TV exec with nothing on his mind bar ratings.

'I'm on my way to the television station now. Are you coming with me? I could do with some moral support, if that's on offer,' Chris said as he swung his jacket over his shoulder and headed for the door.

'Oh, I'm coming,' Adam said. 'But only so that on the drive over there I can do everything in my power to talk you out of it.'

'OK, but you're not coming into the meeting with me,' Chris said. 'You're too bloody good-looking. They'll forget about me in a heartbeat and do everything they can to snap you up instead.'

'Don't panic, mate,' Adam drawled. 'I wouldn't be in your shoes for the world.'

Cara checked her lip gloss in her compact mirror for the third time on the cab drive over.

She had dressed conservatively, as she figured that was how they would want her to dress their guy. She wore a vintage black jersey crossover dress and simple silver antique jewellery. Her short curly bob was pulled away from her face and anchored with a large red hibiscus, and her make-up was subtle, all so that nothing could take away from her new red satin Kate Madden Designs shoes, which were expensive enough to make that month's mortgage payments a squeeze.

The feeling of a brick in her chest grew heavier at the recollection of the price she had paid for them. But if she got the job it wouldn't matter—she would be free and clear. And that was the goal she had to keep dangling in front of herself like a carrot in front of a mule.

She closed the compact, smacked her lips together once more and found the taxi driver watching her in the rear-view mirror. She sent him a self-conscious smile.

'Big date?' he asked.

Cara shook her head. 'Job interview.'

'At the TV station? What sort of job? Are you a news-reader or something?'

'No, nothing like that. I'm hoping to land a job on one of those new dating shows. I don't even know the title or anything. It's all pretty hush-hush, actually.'

She jolted forward lightly in her seat as he unexpectedly pumped the brakes.

'Really?' the driver said. 'Are you going to be one of those girls in bikinis who sit in a hot tub all day?'

'Gosh, no!' she declared. 'I'm a behind-the-scenes type. I'm going for the job of styling the male lead in the show.'

'Oh,' the driver said before focussing more fully on the road ahead. Obviously hot tubs and bikinis were much more his scene.

He soon pulled up outside the old concrete building that housed the television studios. Cara hopped out and handed the cash through the driver's side window.

'Good luck,' the driver said. 'And I'll look out for you on the small screen.'

He gave her the once-over and Cara knew he didn't believe her for a second and was happily measuring her up for a bikini. Knowing she looked more like a ballet dancer than a *Baywatch* babe didn't stop her from blushing in humiliation as he gave a little shrug as if to say he'd seen better.

Cara tugged at her born-again dress, patted down her curls, took a deep breath, and headed inside.

Adam sat upstairs in the top-floor foyer of the television station, cracking his knuckles.

He could have waited in the car. He could have browsed in the shop windows near the television station. He could have taken advantage of the heretofore unheard-of spare time and chosen to stop and smell the flowers in the park nearby. But he hadn't. He wanted to be where Chris was. And since Chris had been taken into a closed-door meeting, the foyer was as close as he was going to get.

After a good hour spent counting tiles on the ceiling of the open-plan waiting room Adam was itching to leave. And to take Chris with him. If there was even the slightest hint that Chris might change his mind, Adam wanted to be there to snap him up and take him back to the real world of stock prices and innovative technologies. A quantifiable world that never pretended to be anything other than what it was.

So Adam waited close to the source, his knuckles cracking, his eyes seeking out any movement that passed his way.

Cara checked her reflection in the lift doors.

She lifted a hand to pat down her hair. She was pleased to see the new caramel highlights in her curly chestnut bob gave her the exact hint of sophistication she was after. The huge red flower that held her hair back was securely fastened but still she dug it in deeper. It would be just like her to have the thing fall out of her hair and dangle at an illogical angle down her back for the whole day without her knowing, her intelligence and talent and new caramel highlights becoming blurred behind her often clumsy exterior.

Her best friends called her 'classy Cara' because she was always so put together, but it was also half a joke since they knew what it took for her to be that way.

She looked down at her unforgettable shoes for moral support. It took almost all of her concentration to remain upright, they were so high and delicate. And she was someone who had to lift her feet so as not to trip even when walking in bare feet.

The lift grumbled to a halt on the top floor and her stomach dropped away. At the last minute she closed her eyes, tapped the heels of her red shoes together and made a wish to whichever good fairies might have been listening.

'Let me have this job and I will never want anything else again.'

The lift doors opened, as did her eyes, and she stepped ahead, unforgettable red shoes leading the way.

Adam looked up at the whir of the lift.

A woman exited, walking like a ballerina: head held high, shoulders back, deliberate, as if she had a book on her head and had no intention of letting that book fall.

This woman had enough going for her that Adam stopped cracking his knuckles and let his hands drift to rest casually across the back of the couch.

She stopped outside the lift and checked the staff listings, bending slightly from the waist and affording Adam a nice view of…a very nice view. Seeming satisfied she was in the right place, she walked his way.

Only when she came closer did he notice evidence of nerves. She swallowed too many times, her eyes flitting about the place as if she was cataloguing everything in the room, and her knuckles showed white against the sleek black portfolio she clutched in her hands like a lifeline.

Finally her fluttery gaze cut his way.

She managed half a smile, her smooth full lips kicking up at one side, highlighting the sexiest little smile line along one pale cheek.

'Excuse me,' she said in a charmingly husky voice, 'but is this the place to wait for the guys from…?' She paused, her mouth closing in an adorable little pout as she found the words she was looking for. 'I don't even know what it's called. The new TV dating show?' A concerned crease appeared above her dainty nose as she awaited his answer.

'This is the place,' he said, drawing his eyes from the crease to her blinking eyes. Green, they were, and magnetic. Like a cat's eyes.

'Oh, thank goodness,' she said, a slim hand moving to her chest while her cat's eyes went back to their dazzled flickering. 'I've had one heck of a time finding where to go. Seems it's all so secretive most of the staff in the building knew nothing about it. But after my bumbling efforts I'm sure the whole place knows by now.'

She took a seat on the opposite couch, sitting upright, with her portfolio still clutched in her hands.

'Are you here to be interviewed?' he asked.

'That I am. And I can't believe how nervous I feel. I've never done anything like this before.'

Ready to ask, *Like what exactly?* Adam suddenly realised that this woman could be one of Chris's dates. And his first uncensored thought was that Chris was a lucky guy. Adam shifted in his seat, suddenly feeling a mite uncomfortable in the woman's sparkling presence.

Then he also remembered that none of the women was to know whom they were going to be meeting on the show. Just some guy, some poor slob hankering for a woman. Not his friend Chris; sweet guy and a billionaire.

But the funny thing was this woman seemed like a sweet

girl too. A sweet girl with eyes that deserved a double take and a mouth that begged to be kissed.

Adam shook his head to clear the muddy thoughts. What did it matter that she was seriously attractive? He was only finding himself so quickly riveted by her because of any possible harm she might bring to Chris.

It was a defence mechanism. That was all.

Chris was too nice to know what was best for him and it was Adam's job to look out for the guy. He owed him that much. If not everything.

The door to the offices beyond opened, and a young, hip television-exec type, with unironed clothes and too much gel in his hair, popped his head out.

'Cara Marlowe?'

Adam's lady friend stood up.

'That's me.'

'Great,' the guy said with an encouraging smile. 'Come on through.'

The woman shot Adam a parting grin that included the sexy smile line once more. 'Wish me luck.'

Luck meant that within days this fresh-faced, sweet and seriously compelling woman could be dating his best friend. And he found that all he could say was, 'Go get 'em.'

Cara followed the young guy, whose name was Jeff, through a maze of corridors and cubicles to his office within the bowels of the top floor of the television station.

'Take a seat,' he ordered.

She did.

'Coffee?'

'Ah, no, thanks.' With caffeine in her veins she'd be bouncing off the walls in no time.

'I'm not so good as you,' Jeff said, waving his empty mug at her. 'I'll be back in a sec.'

Cara sat upright on the plain simple chair as she waited for Jeff to return. She stared down at her red shoes, which glistened prettily back at her. And she winced. Jeff had walked ahead of her the whole time and she was sure he had not even glanced at her feet once.

But the guy in the foyer had. She was sure of that. In fact she was sure he had compiled an internal data file of every inch of her, so intense had been his gaze. It was all she had been able to do to keep her footing. New shoes or no new shoes. A guy like that would make any rational woman's knees go weak without even trying.

He had dark wavy hair, intense blue eyes, a solid build, hands that looked as though they could play the piano and change a light bulb. He was a hunk and a half. She wondered briefly what he was doing there, waiting in the foyer where those involved with the new secret show had been told to wait.

What if he was the single guy? The one she might have to style? She pictured him in his immaculate suit with his glossy shoes and his expensive haircut. If he was the one, her job would be redundant. She would have nothing more to do than straighten his tie and run her hands through his hair just before the cameras rolled.

The thought of getting so up close and personal with that particular gentleman made her suddenly uncomfortable. She shifted in her seat, then gave a little laugh out loud. What need would a guy like that have to go on a dating show? He was gorgeous. The strong, silent type. She imagined a wave of horror rolling across those deep blue eyes at the mere suggestion.

An alarm went off somewhere in the building and Cara clicked back to the present and remembered she was meant to be preparing for the most important job interview of her life. That was what she should have been focussed on, not daydreaming about the exact shade of some stranger's blue eyes. But of course she was only thinking about him so much because of the possible boost he could provide her financial status.

It was a survival mechanism. That was all.

Her focus cleared and she saw her red shoes still gleaming up at her. She had more important things to think about then and there than some chance acquaintance with Mr Handsome out there. She had to make a grand impression on Jeff.

She crossed her legs one way but the shoes were still hidden, so she crossed them the other way instead.

She hadn't even heard Jeff return so as she swung her right leg over her left she connected fully with the poor guy's upper thigh. His coffee-cup did a triple back somersault over his desk, trailing steaming milky coffee over everything in its path. The accompanying 'Oof' that sprang from Jeff's mouth told her that the connection had not been a light one. She leapt to her feet, disentangling herself as she went.

'Jeff, I am so sorry! Here, sit down, please.'

She manoeuvred Jeff into her chair, then reached over to place his tilted empty cup upright, as though it made any difference.

'Are you OK?' she asked, her attention zeroing in on the guy who held her financial stability in his hands. Hands which were currently stuffed between his legs.

'Did I hurt you a great deal? What can I do to help?'

He took a few moments to gather his breath before he finally said, 'When can you start?'

'Start what?' she asked, suddenly worried what she might be called upon to do to *help*.

'The job. The gig. The show.'

'I'm hired?' Cara asked, her squeaky voice showcasing her scepticism.

'That you are,' Jeff promised, his breathing returning to normal.

'Don't you want to see my portfolio?'

'No need. We've seen what you can do and you come highly recommended by those who've worked with you, including Maya Rampling of *Fresh* magazine, who seems to think you are, and I quote, ''a gift from the heavens'', and whose help we will certainly need for marketing the show later on. And that's enough for us.'

Cara spun about on the spot but had to right herself against the table when her dainty shoes threatened to give way beneath her.

'So, are you ours for the having?'

'I am all yours, Jeff. You can have me now.'

The young guy glanced up at her with the beginnings of a smile on his face. Cara snapped her mouth shut and waited for the perfectly reasonable response to her unfortunate phrasing, but instead his kind glance hit the floor once more. He shook his head.

'Those are some shoes you're wearing there, Ms Marlowe. And it pains me to imagine what they might have done to me had we not given you the job.'

CHAPTER TWO

'ADAM TYLER, right?' a husky voice called from behind Adam.

Adam turned to find the lovely lady he had met half an hour before. He blinked. It was a delaying tactic. It gave him a moment to size up the opposition or the problem before he spoke. But whereas before the woman was all elegant nerves, now she was all big smiles and gorgeous dimples. And those were qualities in a woman that he had never seen as a problem.

'That's right,' he said, many years of practice masking everything but nonchalance in his laconic voice.

'Well, now, you see I got the job.' She gave him a little curtsy before continuing. 'And I was told that you were the man I needed to see.'

'Excuse me?'

'To get the dirt on our man of the hour.'

He stood up straight, his hands clasped behind his back, and watched as she shifted from one foot to the other, all but dancing on those high red shoes of hers. Then all of a sudden she stopped fidgeting, piercing him with a stare so sharp he couldn't move. He couldn't even blink. He just stood there and waited for the acute green gaze to give him a reprieve.

'Adam Tyler,' she repeated, her bright eyes flashing as the unexpectedly sharp mind behind them whirred to life. 'Head of Marketing for Revolution Wireless?'

He watched her carefully as the cogs and wheels clicked in her mind. Revolution Wireless. Billionaire. Chris. She would have the whole deal figured out in no time. So much for them recruiting ignoramuses.

It slammed into his mind that nobody was meant to know anything about Chris. That was the whole point, the beauty of the idea, that Chris would be an unknown, just a guy meeting a girl. But suddenly that was all disintegrating before him.

And disintegration was just what Adam wanted.

Her gaze drifted away from him as, like a good girl, she put two and two together. 'Chris Geyer. The name was familiar but I couldn't place it before. He's one of your partners, right?'

He decided to keep his mouth shut. Maybe the fates had put her here just for him. Maybe he didn't need to convince Chris. She could be the spanner in the works all on her own.

'So it's not a joke,' she said. '*The Billionaire Bachelor* is not some hook to get a bunch of poor girls all excited only to have the fake Persian rug whipped out from under them. *The Billionaire Bachelor* is the real deal.'

Adam cringed on the inside. If that was to be the title of the show, Chris was dead meat.

But instead of venting his infuriation with internal screams behind closed eyes, Adam paid close attention to the woman before him, anticipating the inevitable moment when those eyes of hers would skitter back his way, lit all the brighter by the glitter of dollar signs. He braced himself, willing her to get it over with. Willing her to show herself as nothing special, as one of the countless many.

Her glance landed upon him, their eyes clashed, and he took in a short anticipatory breath as he looked for the sly smile that would no doubt touch at the corner of that luscious mouth. The tension inside him grew by the second as he waited for her to feed his disenchantment with womankind.

But the moment never came. Instead of a sly smile, there was a furrowed brow and what he guessed were teeth biting at her inner cheek. She wasn't looking at him as the answer to all her hopes and dreams, she was looking at him as though she felt sorry for him. And where he had been prepared to be disenchanted, instead he was stunned.

She finally collected herself and smiled, but her expression was infinitesimally cooler than when she had first burst from the inner room, all coltish legs and curtsies.

'So, anyway,' she said, her tone pleasant but no longer perky, almost as though she preferred to pretend the past two minutes hadn't existed. 'I have been told that the TV station has an account at a lovely little bistro around the corner and I was hoping that I could take you there for lunch.'

'I'm sorry,' Adam said, gathering his wits after being befuddled by her strange response, 'but I don't think that's in the rules of the game.'

Her confusion was evident. She took in a short breath as though ready to question his comment, before she obviously figured it out for herself, her eyes brightening again with the realisation.

'Please! I am not a contestant! The *last* thing I want or need is some brazen, bawdy billionaire breathing down my neck. Funny, though. You're the second man today to think that. What is it about me that screams bikinis and hot tubs, I wonder?' She said it more to herself than to him, but he still took a brief moment to consider the image.

Her conservative outfit did little to hide the long, lean curves and those unbelievable red shoes did things to her legs and her posture that made his mind turn easily to bikinis and hot tubs.

She moved over to the couch and sat down, patting the seat beside her, beckoning him to join her.

If she wasn't a possible love interest for Chris, then who was she? His interest stirred, he did as he was told, sidling over and sitting beside her, one leg hooking up to cross on top of the other and his arms reaching out to lie across the back of the long leather couch.

'I should have done this better,' she said, holding out a slim ringless hand. 'I'm Cara Marlowe.'

He shook her hand, taking a moment to enjoy the crisp, cool contact. But he waited for her to talk. He found that another good tactic. Most people could not leave silence well alone and they were more likely to fill it with interesting information than if they were questioned directly.

'I am going to be Chris's stylist for the duration of the shoot. It will be my job to dress him.'

'Dress him?'

'Choose his outfits,' she explained. She then reached out and touched his knee, her voice affecting the tones of a New York gossip show host. 'Honey, if I had to actually dress the guy, I'd be asking for a lot more money!'

Adam glanced at her slim hand resting on his knee. It felt nice until it recoiled as though scorched, then moved to slap across her unruly mouth.

'Sorry,' she said. 'I'm a tad overexcited right now. First I get the job of a lifetime and then I meet a real live Australian Businessman of the Year. I would love to talk to you about that some time. Sorry. There I go again. Taking liberties with a practical stranger. My tongue tends to have a mind of its own when my adrenalin is off and running.'

. He gave her a slight nod, though he was again quietly stunned. She knew about his award too? And she was obviously a heck of a lot more impressed with that than with his bank balance. In Adam's long experience with women, this one was proving to be more unusual with every word that came from her lovely mouth.

She was an enigma wrapped in a very enticing dress. A girl with a good head on her shoulders, and a seriously charming face to boot. A woman with such a sexy, husky kick to her voice it could lure sailors to dash their ships upon mountains of rock, whose words spoke, not of the expected sly seduction, but of exuberant enthusiasm for her job.

No matter whom Chris was destined to date on the show, it seemed he would have at least one socially aware woman on set with whom to shoot the breeze. Struck curiously dumb by the thought, Adam once more decided it best to let her do the talking.

And she did.

'So, since they will have your friend Chris tied up for the next couple of hours, let's get out of here and have a natter.'

Even despite becoming lost in those expressive eyes, he somehow managed to pick out the pertinent information. A couple of hours until he saw Chris again? If he had to sit in the dull room for a second longer he would explode even if he was in the company of such an engaging woman.

Secondly, Adam knew when a golden opportunity landed in his lap. He couldn't hide the smile that began to warm him from the inside out. She was to be Chris's stylist. Thoughts of Chris in bizarre golfing outfits or excessive amounts of tartan wove their way through his devious mind. If he couldn't convince Chris he was doing the wrong thing, here was the perfect opportunity to interrupt the process from an entirely unrelated angle.

'It seems that you and I are destined to have a lunch date.'

'Excellent,' she said.

Adam stood, holding out an elbow in invitation. 'Well, then, Ms Marlowe, shall we?'

'Only if you call me Cara,' she said, standing, placing a hand lightly in the crook of his offered arm. Her beguiling smile giving him a third reason to accept the lunch offer with increasing pleasure.

Cara watched Adam from the corner of her eye as she perused the large menu in the lovely little bistro around the corner.

I am having lunch with Adam Tyler, she thought, knowing she would rather be picking his brains about his business practices than about his friend.

As a connoisseur of stories about locals made good, she knew the highlights of his career as reported inside and outside of the business pages. Inside were tales of a marketing guru, part-owner of the fastest growing company in Australia. Awards and plaudits followed in his wake like tin cans clattering along behind a wedding car. Outside the business pages he was more well known for being a playboy-billionaire type, not quite hip enough to make it onto the cover of any of the supermarket gossip magazines, but certainly fascinating enough to grace their social pages time and again.

No wonder too. In the flesh he was pretty darned gorgeous. He oozed manliness, from the woodsy scent of his aftershave, to the easy way he wore his suits. From the practised nonchalance of every effortless movement, to the fact that that very nonchalance could not cover up the fact that his mind did not miss a beat behind those fierce, hooded eyes. Beneath the cool exterior beat the pulse of a brilliant, shrewd, powerful man to whom success on every front would have come all too easily.

And all she'd been able to do was go goo-goo and paw him and talk about bikinis and hot tubs. It was not exactly the impression she would have hoped to make on someone whose business acumen she greatly admired.

She found him looking her way, his eyes faintly questioning, and she knew she had been caught staring. She shot him a big cheesy grin, then went back to flicking through the menu.

The last thing she wanted was to be turning all gooey over some guy with money. And a billionaire? That was entirely out of the question. Money meant power. Money meant control. And Cara was not about to give any of her hard-earned power and control away.

Especially to one who, above and beyond the whole gorgeous, blue-eyed, strapping, silent man thing, was so obviously involved in *The Billionaire Bachelor* project against his will. He was trouble in a three-piece suit. No doubt about it.

'You made up your mind?' Adam asked.

'You bet I have,' she said, her voice deep with determination.

Then after a few seconds of ensuing silence she looked up to find the waiter smiling blandly at her. She quickly picked the first thing that came into focus to cover up the fact that she'd had no idea Adam had been asking about the meal.

'So how does this all work?' Adam asked once they had settled and begun their starters.

Cara opened her mouth to answer but then Jeff's smiling face popped into her mind. 'Tell a soul a thing and you will be out on your backside,' he had said. 'Great recommendations or not.'

'Sorry,' Cara said, 'I'm not sure what I can really tell you. My contract has confidentiality clauses up the wazoo.'

'You've already given away the title of the show.'

Her hands flew to cover her warming cheeks. 'Oh, heavens, I have, haven't I? I'm going to blow this before it even starts. You have permission to stuff a napkin in my mouth if I let it run away from me again.'

'Thank you,' Adam said, 'that's always worth knowing.' He eyed her warily over his herb bread. 'Anyway, I don't mean about the show itself. I know more than I would like to about all that. I was wondering about specifics. For example, will Chris be at work tomorrow?'

'Well, I guess I can tell you that it will take about two weeks. By tomorrow morning at the latest, all of those involved will be sequestered in the Ivy Hotel in the city. And nobody will be able to come and go unless authorised by the producers.'

She watched for Adam's reaction to this news. When Jeff had told her she had all but freaked out, her mind running over with everything she would have to do that night to get her regular life up to date before she disappeared from the face of the earth. But this guy merely nodded and blinked and she had no idea if he was happy or sad or freaking out behind those dark blue eyes.

'Why will you be sequestered, do you think?' he asked.

'To keep any of us from blabbing to the press.'

'About what?'

'The juicy details. The name of the show...'

Adam smiled and it was all Cara could do to go on, the charming appeal it brought to his strong face was so unexpected.

'The star of the show,' she continued. 'The fact there even is a show. When word gets out, the producers want to control the spin. I've worked in the fashion biz for a

number of years now and what it boils down to is the fact
that sex sells. Television is sexy. Secrets are sexy. There is
nothing sexier to eighteen-to-thirty-five-year-old women
than a man so in tune with himself that he is openly looking
for love. And the producers of the show want to reap the
benefits.'

She finished her statement with a deep intake of breath.
Now she was certain of it. The way he was watching her,
weighing her words so carefully—this guy had ulterior mo-
tive written all over him. He smiled easily enough, and his
body language certainly showed that he was open to anything she had to offer. *Any conversation topic,* she thought,
giving herself a mental slap. But if for some reason he
wanted this all to go away, she was pretty sure he would
have his way. And it made her so nervous her chest hurt.

It sure didn't help her nerves that he continued to be just
as unreservedly attractive as he was when she first laid eyes
on him. It would have been more helpful for her jitters if
he slouched, or fixed his hair an inordinate number of
times, or if he professed a predilection for polka music.

She took a sip of water to stem the urge to babble and
her mind whizzed back, hoping desperately she had not said
anything idiotic or anything she shouldn't have. She was
pretty sure she had done well. 'That's all I'm prepared to
tell,' she said. 'Sorry.'

He shrugged. A movement so slight she didn't know if
he'd really shrugged at all or if she'd just caught his es-
sential indifference.

'OK, then, back to the reason why we're here,' Cara said,
deciding it was about time she took control of the conversation if she was to get anything useful out of him. 'Tell
me about Chris.'

'What would you like to know?' Adam asked.

'What does he look like, for starters?' Though Adam was

recognisable to her, she could not have picked the other owners of Revolution Wireless out of a line-up if her job depended on it.

Adam blinked. She had already pegged the fact that he did that when he was biding his time. Cara bit her bottom lip. Time-biding was not on her list of most favourite things.

'Does he look anything like you, for instance?'

'In some ways, yes. In other ways not at all.'

'I see,' she said. 'And what does he do for fun?'

This time the blink was different. It was loaded with thought. But she knew not what about.

'He creates telecommunications innovations,' Adam finally said.

Her lip-biting increased to a calorie-burning rate.

'OK. So how do you two know each other? Just from work? What rings his bells? What sort of woman do you think he is trying to land?'

Give me anything, please!

'We know each other from school.'

She waited for more but…nothing came.

'Fantastic,' she said, her patience finally running down. Sure, she had the job, but the last thing she needed was for it to work out so badly that she never worked again. Even with a mortgage paid off, a girl had city council rates and amenities to keep her working ad infinitum. And this guy had nothing to offer her but a bit of a crush.

'Well, that's all I needed,' she said, refolding her napkin and making ready to leave. 'Now I know he looks exactly yet nothing like you, he invents stuff for a living and he once went to school, I'm all set. With those specifics in mind I can now make sure he doesn't look like a complete dud for the millions of people who will watch him eagle-eyed every week.'

'Wait,' Adam said, his hand landing atop hers.

Cara let out a nervous breath, seriously glad her bluff had worked. She sat down slowly and shot him her best blasé expression, but she knew already she was up against a professional in that department.

This time she waited for him to talk. If she was sitting with the best she might as well learn from him. And after a few seconds of duelling silence she realised that his hand was still atop hers.

Her gaze flittered down. His hand captured her attention once again. It was big and broad and tanned, especially lying on top of her own, which was small and pale. As she stared the silence changed. It became thick and noisy with unuttered complications.

Slowly she slipped her hand away and he didn't stop her. She bit her lip to bring herself back to the present, then looked him straight in the eye and said, 'Adam, please tell me about your friend so I can make this as easy for him as I can.'

Adam had been ready to convince the girl to have Chris decked out with spats and a walking stick if that was what it would take to have his friend give up the game. But with her looking at him like that, beseeching, pleading, he found himself wilting. He told himself it was only because she made a good point.

It was in her power to make Chris look like an idiot. And when she had asked what Chris did for fun, Adam had baulked because he knew that Chris did nothing. Chris had worked tirelessly for years to achieve their joint goal, and now he was simply asking for some 'him' time. Didn't he deserve at least that much?

'So you really don't know what he looks like?' Adam asked.

She shook her head, slowly, as though if she went any

faster he would not be able to keep up. 'Nope. Not a bit. I have no idea if he's old, young, thin, fat, balding or has a glorious head of hair.'

It was fair enough that she didn't. Come to think of it, he was the only one who seemed to end up in any of those other types of magazines, the ones that the guys at work liked to snip out and stick on the corkboard in the kitchenette.

Cara blinked at him, her lashes sweeping down onto her cheeks in a look that spoke of pure and simple time-biding. And it took him a second to recover. He had to remind himself of the good-head-behind-the-pretty-face theory he had stumbled onto earlier.

Adam shifted in his seat, unused to being on the receiving end of his own tricks. This woman was a quick learner and he knew then and there he would have to stay on his toes. If this was to go smoothly for Chris, and thus work out to Revolution Wireless's best advantage, he would have to keep a close eye on this one.

'OK, then,' Adam began, 'first things first, Chris ain't anywhere near brazen, so wipe that idea out right now. Picture a man...'

Cara leant forward, resting her chin on the heel of her palms as the guy across the table gave a rundown of the life and times of Chris Geyer. Stories of childhood antics, of bad dates, of a love of education, of a twenty-year friendship ran thick and fast. Cara listened with half an ear, smiling in all the right places, building up the idea of a friendly teddy-bear type whom she was more and more looking forward to meeting.

But the other half of her mind was focussed on the man telling the story. All efforts at nonchalance put aside, he became a charismatic, vibrant story-teller. Her nerves dissolved with every captivating word and she couldn't take her eyes off him.

She could tell that he usually hid behind his laconic attitude so that he could measure the world without it measuring him. But behind the attitude lurked the guy who ran one of the most successful marketing campaigns the country had ever seen. This was the guy who could sell cookies to Girl Guides, he was just that compelling.

As she often did when she met new people, Cara pictured how she would light him. If ever, one day, she had the chance to do so, it would be all about shadows, taking advantage of those fantastic cheekbones and that straight nose. She would brush his hair back a tad further, knowing that he would only curl up more inside himself and make himself that much more intriguing. The carefully constructed remoteness, the seriously attractive mystery, the gorgeous depths of those navy-blue eyes...

'Don't you need to take any notes?' Adam asked, his hands stopping mid-demonstration of how a mobile phone was built.

Cara snapped back to the present with such a jolt, her elbow slipped off the table and she had to catch herself before her chin followed in its wake.

'Are you OK?' he asked, lifting from his seat, reaching for her, his expression bright with surprise.

Bad. Bad Cara. What on earth had she been doing, daydreaming like that? Her attention had become wrapped in the words of some strapping stranger when her focus for the next two weeks should be blissfully caught up in the ins and outs of the most challenging and significant job of her life.

'Yes, I'm fine,' she said. 'And no as well. I don't need to take notes. Really.' She jabbed furiously at her temple. 'All stored up here.'

'So are you a Cary Grant fan?' he asked as he poured her a glass of wine.

Cara fought to remember a single word of his conversation and came up blank. 'A who…what?'

Adam's eyes narrowed. 'Cary Grant. Chris's favourite actor? He's in *The Philadelphia Story*, *His Girl Friday*…'

Cara shook her head hard to clear out the soft and fuzzies that had gathered therein. 'Sure. Of course. I love Cary Grant. I think he's marvellous. I can even do an impression if you'd like.'

'No need. Really.'

She fully deserved Adam's bemused smile.

'So to recap, Chris is a great guy who loves Cary Grant, collects bells—'

'Shells,' Adam corrected, pouring himself a glass of wine.

'Shells,' she said without missing a beat. 'And shells… sells telephones for a living.'

Adam nodded slowly. 'In a nutshell, yes. And he deserves a toast, don't you think, for being the one to bring us together for this lovely lunch?'

'Who?' Cara asked, the soft and fuzzies winning hands down. 'Cary Grant?'

Adam laughed, his head shaking, his eyes bright with amused confusion. 'Why the heck not?' He lifted his glass. 'To Cary Grant.'

Cara had had enough. Another second of this conversation and she would probably forget her own name. She stood, dropped her napkin to the arm of her chair and then didn't know where to put her hands. 'You've been a fantastic help, but it's time for me to be…elsewhere. Thanks for lunch. And I guess I'll…see you 'round like a rissole!'

Before she could plant her foot deeper in her mouth Cara took off. She weaved through the tightly packed restaurant tables with her mind on the task ahead. Get to the television station. Meet Chris. Do the best job she could. Keep said job. Take home pay. Own St Kilda Storeys. So long as she kept that mantra going through her head, she was unstoppable. Surely?

Adam Tyler and his dreamy, distracting blue eyes did not come into the mantra once, so the bigger the distance between the two of them, the better.

Adam remained seated, debating internally whether it was better to watch her walk away, her lithe hips swinging as she mastered her outrageous shoes, or to watch her from front on, her lovely face so animated, her hands forever moving with nervous energy, and that huge flower bouncing about atop her head.

He dragged his interest away with some regret.

So, it looked as though Chris was going to be *The Billionaire Bachelor*. He cringed again. But that would have to be the last time. He had no choice. He was going to have to join bloody Chris on the set for the next two bloody weeks and act as babysitter to his bloody best friend.

'Sex sells,' Cara had said. He knew she was spot on. And if that feisty employee was anything to go by, he had the unsettling but mounting feeling that this show was going to produce fireworks...and that it would be in Revolution Wireless's interest to be seen to be lighting the match.

CHAPTER THREE

CARA went home to St Kilda Storeys, her beloved apartment building that would very soon be truly hers. There was a note from Gracie on her apartment door. She took the steps, two at a time, to Gracie's top-floor apartment and knocked.

Cara heard scuffling and snuffling as Minky got to the door first. Gracie was looking after the fluffy, almost-white, Maltese Terrier while their fellow Saturday Night Cocktails gang member Kelly and her husband Simon were out of town visiting friends in Fremantle.

Gracie finally opened the door with a wriggling Minky in her arms. 'Well?' she said.

'I got the job.'

Cara was lost in hugs from Gracie, and tiny lapping kisses from Minky.

'I knew it!' Gracie said. 'Or at least I wished and hoped super hard!'

Gracie grabbed Cara and steered her toward the small old couch that took up half of the tiny lounge. 'I have ten minutes before I have to be at work. So tell me all about…everything.'

'I can't, actually. It's all seriously under wraps.'

'Even to me?'

'Especially to you.'

Gracie had the good grace to nod. 'Good plan. I can't keep a secret to save my life. Keep it to yourself. So tell me something else. Who did you meet? Anybody famous?

How about that guy who hosts the movie review programme? He's a bit of a hottie.'

'Wrong channel.'

'Oh, yeah, right. Anyone else I can brag about?'

'Umm, not really. Though you'll be pleased to know that
I did have an interesting lunch with this one guy…'

Cara went on to fill Gracie in on the important points of
her lunch date—no names mentioned, of course: the ominous stare, the powerful grace, the serious good looks worthy of a menswear catalogue.

'Armani or Target?' Gracie asked, using their usual
scale.

'Armani, without a doubt.'

Gracie nodded in pleasant surprise. But either way the
truth about this guy was immaterial. Cara was going to be
holed up in a hotel for the next two weeks with way too
much else to occupy her to care.

Adam went back to work.

Dean, the third partner in the Revolution Wireless giant,
was pacing behind his desk. Where Chris was the ideas
guy, and Adam was the salesman, Dean looked after the
day-to-day blood, sweat and tears side of the operation, and
it showed. His tie was long gone and his shirt sleeves were
rolled up, his hands flying about him as he yabbered away
into a telephone head set.

Adam took a seat at the desk and waited for the one-
sided staccato conversation to finish.

'Adam, my man,' Dean said, giving his friend a hearty
handshake, before resuming his pacing. 'What's up?'

'It's about Chris.'

'And this dating show deal?'

Adam nodded.

Dean flapped a dismissive hand across his face. 'Let him be.'

'Are you serious?'

'Sure. It's been over a year since he last took a holiday, so think of it that way if it helps.'

'It doesn't help. I have worked my backside off to sell Revolution Wireless as a serious company, as serious competition against the giants who have cornered the market for years, and just as we've made the leap Chris is about to go and make us all look like amateurs.'

'Not amateurs,' Dean said, eyeing Adam down. 'Human. And human ain't such a bad angle to give a company this size, if you ask me.'

Adam blinked and Dean cocked an eyebrow at the move.

'So you back him on this?' Adam asked.

'A hundred per cent. I think he's a brave, brave fellow. He's putting it all out there and that takes guts. And I don't see why Revolution Wireless should suffer for showing that one of our leading lights has guts to spare.'

Adam let the idea wash over him. He was being shot down from all angles and he knew it would not do anybody any good if he fought against such diminishing odds.

'OK, then. If that's your decision, I want us to sponsor the show.'

Dean stopped his pacing at once. He ran a hand through his sandy hair, though it fell back into the same shambles instantly. 'You want us to sponsor the show?'

'Well, it certainly looks like I can't stop the show, so why not make the most of it? Why not take advantage of the fact that it will be a significantly supported prime-time television event with the opportunity for intensive branding that is set to rake in viewing numbers like none other has done before?'

And that way he could wangle his way onto the set, insist

that he be able to stay in the hotel with the cast and crew, because only then could he keep an eye on Chris. Make sure his magnanimous friend did not lose his heart and along with it his wallet to some conniving, manipulative schemer. Because for the life of him he could not see how the whole episode could end any other way.

Dean's smile dawned slowly. 'Sure, why not? You're the marketing guru, my friend, so if you think it will float, you have my vote.'

Adam nodded. Decision made. 'So will you be OK with the two of us AWOL for the next couple of weeks?'

'Of course. So long as you're on the other end of the phone. I mean, if *we* couldn't run our business by mobile phone and email we would be in a heap of trouble!'

Adam could not help but smile. 'Too true.'

Three of Dean's phone lines lit up almost simultaneously.

Adam stood. 'I'll leave you to it.'

Dean nodded, and his pacing resumed. He gave Adam a brief wave as he left the room.

Cara had her assistant offload the couple of jobs she had pencilled in for the next fortnight. But she called her main client, Maya Rampling, the editor of *Fresh* magazine, herself.

'Cara, darling! I hear congratulations are in order!'

'Maya, you are the darling. I know you're half the reason I got this job. Even though it means I have had to pass the styling of your lingerie shoot onto a colleague.'

'I will miss your light touch, Cara, but don't give it another thought. This job was simply made for you.'

'Did they call you or did you call them?'

'Darling, they would be afraid for me to find out *anything* after everyone else. Just take this one piece of advice.

Watch your back. TV jobs are notoriously precarious. Half the crew will be turned around by the end of the shoot. It's like the big boys are so scared of losing their jobs themselves, they have to keep everyone else on their toes.'

'OK…' Cara felt the brick in her chest grow a kilogram heavier.

'So be good. Keep your head down. Don't cause trouble. Do your job with a minimum of fuss and you'll be fine. Above all have fun, and I'll see you soon.'

Then Maya hung up.

Have fun? Cara thought. With those last pieces of advice hanging over her she would be afraid to smile at the wrong person in case she did the wrong thing. No. She would keep her head down and do her job. She would keep her job and she would pay off her mortgage. Her mantra well and truly re-established, she felt ready again.

She showered, changed into cut-off denim jeans, a white collared T-shirt and white flat Mary-Janes, closed her suitcase, checked all the electrics at home were shut off, and then left.

A big black limousine awaited her at the front door. She wound down the window so she could have a good look at her old red stucco building. A smattering of coloured perennials swayed lightly in the front garden. Lights shone from most of the windows. Music spilled from a second-floor apartment. The next time she would see it, she would own it outright.

The car took off, its engine humming softly. They drove past girls in G-string bikinis parading the beach. Boys lined the walkways, acting as though they were simply pausing to check out the ships in the distance, but the girls in the G-string bikinis knew better.

It drove Cara to wonder about the mysterious Chris Geyer, putting himself on the line for love. She wondered what it would take for someone to go to that sort of length to find themselves a partner.

She, who had never considered going on a dating show, had never looked up an internet dating agency, had only gone to nightclubs for the dancing with her friends, simply could not see herself in his shoes. When it came down to it she knew she was actually spending a good deal of time *not* looking to find herself a partner.

Still, no matter what Chris's reasons were, they had afforded her the opportunity of a lifetime and for that she would be for ever indebted to his romantic nature. So long as the anti-romantic nature of his friend did not turn the idea sour.

As the big car turned towards the city, Cara sank back into the soft seat feeling as if the rest of her life were waiting around the next corner.

'It's a done deal,' Adam said as he shook hands with Jeff of the unironed clothes and the too much hair gel. 'Revolution Wireless will be the main sponsor of this series of *The Billionaire Bachelor* and as such I will be allowed access to all areas of the set.'

'So long as you stay at the hotel,' Jeff qualified, 'and are bound by the same rules as the rest of us for the next two weeks, that's fine.'

Adam shot the younger man a wry smile. 'Of course. That went without saying.'

'Yet I said it anyway,' Jeff said, returning the smile. 'So if you can be at the hotel by eight o'clock tonight we will have a room for you—'

'On the same floor as Chris.'

'You will have the suite next door,' Jeff agreed. 'So here is a copy of the schedule, a timetable of the events that will occur within the confines of the show.'

Adam flicked through the document, which had no header and no front page. If anyone on the street found it they would think it a terribly dull, unimportant business memo, not the breakdown of the best-kept secret in Australian television.

'*The Billionaire Bachelor* is going to be huge,' Jeff promised. 'You won't regret this.'

No matter that Adam was now officially one of the gang, all the connotations implied by that title still made him fume. Chris sure needed him if he was going to come through this ordeal unscathed. And if Adam had anything to do with it, his friend would come out of this a billionaire and a bachelor still.

The front doors of the Ivy Hotel were guarded with big burly bouncers and a metal detector. They scanned the bar-code on Cara's pass and let her through the doors. Once inside, a whole other set of security guards searched her luggage for recording equipment and found only a Polaroid camera, which was listed against her name as an allowable item. The place was really locked down tight. And she was being let through to the inner sanctum. Her whole body hummed with excitement and she hoped it had nothing to do with the metal detectors.

And then her suitcase began to ring.

The security guard, whose nametag read "Joe Buck, li-cence number 2483", had been about to pass over her case and let her through. But at the ringing he tightened his grip. 'I'm sorry, Ms Marlowe, but mobile phones are not allowed as per your contract.'

They had a brief game of tug of war before Cara let go. 'But I didn't bring my phone,' she said, sure she had left it at home on her ironing-board.

Her case stopped ringing.

They looked at each other for a moment, both kind of hoping the other would agree that maybe they had imagined it.

'OK, then, Ms Marlowe,' Joe the security guard said. He handed the suitcase over again before the ringing resumed. 'Ms Marlowe, I'm terribly sorry, but—'

Cara felt herself blushing to her toes. 'I know. I know. I'm sorry. Just give me a second. I really do not remember packing it.'

With Maya's words—*keep your head down, don't cause trouble, minimum of fuss*—ringing in her head, she wanted to get this spectacle over with as quickly as possible. She lobbed her suitcase onto the ground, bent from the waist, unzipped the case, peeked around her neatly folded clothes and found...nothing.

A distinctive murmur invaded her ears. She glanced between her knees and saw a line had formed behind her. What a fantastic first impression she was making on her new colleagues: bum in the air, being searched for contraband.

The ringing stopped. She shook her case and the ringing began all over again. Not having any luck with checking under her clothes with care, she began to scoop them out in a flurry, hanging them messily over her shoulder. Her just-washed hair kept hanging in her eyes and she had to constantly blow it out of her face. Added to that she was getting hot from the unusual lifting movements that felt agonisingly like exercise. She was in first-day-on-the-job hell.

'Is everything all right here?'

At the sound of the familiar deep voice, Cara stood up so fast the blood took longer than necessary to reach her head. She held out a hand to steady herself as the world turned fuzzy and black. Since Adam Tyler was the closest pillar to hand, he had to do.

Her vision slowly cleared. She looked into her nemesis's dark blue eyes and bit back a self-effacing groan. He would hardly want to talk seriously about his time as Australian Businessman of the Year with a woman who could barely put one foot in front of the other without something going awry.

It just wasn't fair that she had to be at her most klutzy around someone so smooth. Her last words to him had been 'see you 'round like a rissole,' for goodness' sake! Who said that bar eight-year-olds and grown-ups with limited sophistication?

It only made him all the more intimidating and she did not stand for feeling that way with anyone. She was talented. She was sought after. She was focussed. She was ambitious. She was self-made. She was leaning against him, her hand splayed across his unexpectedly sculpted chest, with half her clothes strewn over her shoulder and a pair of plain white cotton panties hanging from her finger.

She whipped her hand away and tucked it behind her, shaking madly until the underwear plopped back into her suitcase.

'Are you OK?' he asked, reaching out to take her by the shoulder as though he was afraid she might collapse atop his shiny shoes.

Finding herself flummoxed, she pulled away, crouched down and began to pile her clothes back into her suitcase.

'Low blood pressure,' she said, frantically shoving her entire collection of cotton pants that had managed to make their way out of her suitcase back into her suitcase. 'Stood up too fast. Should have known better. Gives me blackouts.'

'Ah, Ms Marlowe,' Joe the security guard cut in. 'Your mobile phone?'

She threw the rest of her clothes atop the suitcase and stepped away. 'You look for it. Please. Be my guest.'

The guard looked to Adam as though hoping perhaps he would prefer to rifle through her intimates instead. Adam backed behind Cara. But then the ringing sound returned and the guard took a deep breath and went searching.

As Cara watched in mortified silence, it finally occurred to her that she was once again in the vicinity of the man she had been looking forward to never seeing again.

'What are *you* doing here anyway?' she asked under her breath.

'You're the one who needed the leaning post,' he said from right behind her.

'Not here. But *here*, in the hotel.'

At that moment Joe the security guard came up with something jingling in his hand. It was not a mobile phone. It was a card. It had a huge 'CONGRATULATIONS!' scrawled across the front. And when the guard opened it the card played a very good imitation of a mobile phone ring tone.

Cara, Adam, and a good number of those in line craned over the guard's shoulder for a closer look, to find the long gushy note Gracie had written and hidden in her case before Cara had left.

Every one of the big burly men turned to Cara with mushy looks on their faces. Cara just tapped her foot and held out a hand. Blushing, Joe handed over her private mail.

'I am terribly sorry, Ms Marlowe.'

'That's OK, Joe,' she said, swallowing down her indignation and embarrassment. There was no reason to make him feel bad. He hadn't done anything wrong, though Gracie would receive a tongue-lashing along with a hug for this particular stunt. Cara gave the guard a pat on the back and smiled until she sensed him relaxing. 'You were doing your job. And with impressive thoroughness. You are a credit to your post.'

Joe blushed and scuffed his toe on the carpet.

'Can I have my case now?' Cara asked.

'Sure. Of course.' Joe returned to his packing with extra special care.

Cara cleared her throat. 'Thanks, Joe, but I can look after it from here.'

Joe stood up, his blush growing by the second. While he went back to checking the bags of the growing line of guests, Cara continued to repack her case. But of course she could no longer get it closed. She looked about her for help. Joe was going through Adam's bag and naturally everything seemed to be going swimmingly for him.

Adam glanced her way. She bit back her pride and waved him over. 'If I sit, can you zip?'

A knowing smile lifted his mouth and she wanted nothing more than to slap it away. 'Of course,' he said.

She sat, having to lift her legs when he rounded the front, so that he could duck beneath them. Would there never be an end to her humiliation when he was about?

'Come on, say it,' she insisted.

'What?'

'Whatever it is you're thinking.' *Some smartypants comment about my backside, or falling into your arms, or about my white cotton underwear.*

'I was thinking you handled Joe's embarrassment brilliantly. You are one very nice lady, Ms Marlowe.'

'Oh.'

Adam tugged the zip through the last few centimetres. Taking a hold of her ankles, he pulled her feet back to the ground. 'There. All done.'

He kept a hold of her bare ankles for several long moments before releasing his grip with a final soft pat. Cara had to swallow to wet her suddenly parched throat.

'Adam, you never did say what you were doing here?'

'Not surprisingly, considering the floor show was a heck of a lot more interesting than anything I had to say.'

Cara felt a growl growing in her chest but Adam got there first.

'Revolution Wireless is sponsoring the show.'

Now that statement deserved a hesitant blink.

'Wow. That's some turn-round. At lunch I could have sworn you thought the show the most ludicrous idea you had ever come across.'

'I did. And I still do. But, nevertheless, people who know more about these sorts of things than I do tell me that it will be the biggest thing on television bar the Aussie Rules Grand Final. So I am here as Revolution Wireless's representative.'

'For the whole two weeks?' Cara asked, trying to rein in her hysterical voice.

He nodded.

'Mr Tyler,' the security guard called out. 'Mobile phone, laptop, printer, all on the list. You're right to go through.'

Adam watched her for a few moments longer before standing and returning to his bags without another word.

Seeing her chance to retire as gracefully as possible, Cara stood, and dragged her suitcase to the lift as quickly as she could.

Adam watched her walk away.

The woman was good entertainment value if nothing else. He watched her shuffle from one foot to the other as though the floor were covered in hot coals, and then as the lift doors slowly opened she bolted like a cat with her tail on fire.

Joe the security guard cleared Adam to go on through into the hotel proper. Adam sauntered to the lift recalling what a cute tail it was, squeezed into pale denim cut-offs that had been washed so many times they fit her like second skin. Though she was a slim woman, she certainly curved just where she ought. He had been well aware of that when walking up to the front door of the hotel and seeing those very curves wiggling so engagingly at him.

The moment he had realised just whose curves they were, he had instantly jumped in to help. Or, if he was honest with himself, he had instantly leapt to shield her considerable temptations from appreciative eyes other than his own.

Who needs security guards in this place? he joked to himself. *Adam Tyler is on the scene and he's ready and willing to protect everybody from themselves.*

CHAPTER FOUR

CARA was up early the next morning. She hustled down-stairs to the buffet for some peace and quiet as she had the distinct feeling that it would be the last she would get for a good two weeks. It had nothing to do with avoiding one particular member of the crew, of course. She was happy to avoid all of them after her grand entrance the night before.

On her way back to her room, Cara passed by a young woman in sweaty gym gear who could not for the life of her get her door unlocked.

'Do you need a hand?' Cara asked.

The woman looked up, her pale blue eyes flashing. 'I can't seem to work this stupid card thing. I only arrived this morning and the guy who carried my bags let me in the first time.'

Cara held out her hand. 'May I?'

The woman gave it over as though it were a hot potato. 'Please. Otherwise I may be going about my day looking like this.' She pulled out a hunk of lanky hair, damp from an obvious session at the gym downstairs.

'Well, I wouldn't wish that on any of my fellow women,' Cara said, sliding the card through the slot. The door opened without a problem.

'You can't hardly tell I'm a country girl, can you?' the woman said with a self-deprecating smile, and her best hick accent. 'How's a gal like me meant to figure out one of these fandangled big city doohickies? Back home we don't even have front doors!'

'Don't worry about it,' Cara said with a smile. 'I've been here since last night so I've had time to master all the fandangled doohickies.'

'Practice makes perfect, then?'

'That's it.'

'Well, thanks…' The woman smiled at Cara with her head cocked to one side.

'Cara,' Cara said.

'Thanks, Cara. I'm Maggie. Anyway, I'd better get on in there and get my fire started so I can cook me some tucker.'

Cara could not help but laugh. The young woman was such a sweetheart. 'Put on a sausage for me.'

'Shall do. See ya!'

Cara didn't even make it to her room before Jeff was on the scene. She had already swiped her card so Jeff just bundled in after her, chattering away about the plans for the day.

'Do you mind if I go to the bathroom by myself?' she asked, half joking but half making sure he wasn't about to follow her in there.

'Go for it,' he said. 'Just listen up as you go.'

'OK, then.'

He sat on her bed and she was glad she was a naturally tidy person. The idea of this guy having to move last night's underwear from her bed didn't appeal. Especially since half the crew had already had a good gander the night before.

Cara did her make-up and cleaned her teeth as Jeff happily yabbered away. 'So today you get to meet Chris. Outfit him. Make him as hunky as you can. And tonight he meets the girls.'

She popped her head around the door to find him reading the last page of the book by her bed.

'Any good?' he asked.

She shook her head to try to keep up with him. 'Did you say we start shooting tonight?'

'Yep. So you'd better get cracking. Collect Chris upstairs in Suite 44, then straight downstairs to collect your credit card and limo. Shop, shop, shop. And I'll see you back by midday so we can dress him, mike him, and paint him.'

Then Jeff bounced off as quickly as he had arrived. Cara hastened her ablutions, then headed upstairs.

She knocked on the door for Suite 44 and a butler escorted her into a gorgeous suite five times the size of her own room.

The room opened up into a sunken lounge with a bar, and assorted gym equipment scattered across a raised platform by the ceiling-to-floor windows. The carpet felt so soft beneath her feet she itched to reach down and run her fingers through it. It would have been a great location for the underwear shoot she had been set to style for *Fresh* magazine, but she had to bite back that idea. Too late now. She had made her bed. She would simply remember the location for next time.

'Hello,' she called out. 'Anybody home?'

She stopped peering around corners and stood bolt upright when Adam Tyler, in his ubiquitous suit and tie, sauntered out of one of the opened doorways off to her right.

Her face warmed instantly under his unexpected gaze. Whatever for, she had no idea.

'Oh, I am sorry,' she said, backing away. 'I must have the wrong room.'

'You're looking for Chris?' he asked, his deliberate, sexy voice stopping her short.

'I am.'

He kept walking her way and she just stood there, rooted to the spot, as his personal magnetism washed over her in waves. She wondered if Chris would be such a terrible force. If so, it would make for a suffocating atmosphere.

'He won't be a moment,' Adam said, veering off towards the bar. 'Why don't you take a seat? Would you like a coffee?'

Cara shook her head. It took enough effort to keep her balance, mentally and physically, in the presence of this guy; she didn't think she needed caffeine to make it worse.

From behind Adam came a man of about the same age, mid-thirties or so. It had to be Chris. And Cara was infinitely glad to see that he was nowhere near as intimidating a figure as Adam: he was sweet and sandy-looking, like a day at the beach. He gave her a little finger wave then drew a finger to his lips, hushing her from alerting Adam to his presence. Cara bit her lip and drew her amused gaze back to Adam.

Sensing at once she had an ally, she felt her confidence return tenfold. She walked over to Adam, keen to keep his attention on her and not his silent friend.

'So, Adam, now we have established I am where I am meant to be, may I ask what *you* are doing here so bright and early? Don't you have somewhere else to be? Sponsorship deals to wangle? Million-dollar ad campaigns to oversee?'

Sensing Adam was about to turn and find Chris behind him, Cara dug deep for something that would make him stop. 'Or don't you have some buxom blonde to dump?' she asked.

That did it! Adam turned back her way with his usual slow grace. He watched her carefully, like a tiger who was not quite hungry enough to chase her down, but who saw her as a possible morsel for later just the same.

'Now where did you get that idea?' he asked.

'Oh, I don't know.' Cara flitted a hunted gaze to Chris

who gave an encouraging two thumbs up. So on she went. 'Isn't that what you are most famous for? Blondes first, billions second?'

After a few watchful moments, he shrugged. 'No blondes to dump right at this moment, so here I am.'

He turned away and for some reason it irked that he didn't seem to mind her comments in the least. She breathed deep, fortifying herself against his nonchalance.

'You really don't need to be, I'm sure. You'd think your friend couldn't tie his shoes without you.'

'Well, maybe he can't,' Adam said and Chris doubled over as though he'd been stabbed in the heart.

'Well, maybe you should give him the chance to try,' Cara said.

'Well, maybe it's best for him to keep his mind on more important details like running a multibillion-dollar business.'

'Well, maybe he thinks there are more important things than money.'

'Well, maybe your real concern is, with me here, you don't get to tie his shoelaces and that puts you out of a job. So who has the real money concern here, do you think?'

Electricity flickered across the room. She could feel it in every nerve ending. She was pretty sure she would be able to fling him across the room with a bolt of lightning shot from her fingertips if she really wanted to.

Then she pulled herself up. What was she doing baiting the guy like that? It had all begun as a little joke. All she'd wanted to do was keep him from finding out his friend was listening in.

She was a conciliator. She was a diplomat. She was the one to stop an argument, not to hold up her fists and shout, 'Bring it on!' Especially to a guy who looked as though he could wipe the mat with her. But there was just something about him that rubbed her the wrong way. He made her squabble muscles itch.

'Well, maybe you two should get a room!' Chris finally shouted.

Adam spun to face him and Cara was able to stand down. She unclenched her fists and rolled her shoulders, feeling ridiculously like a prize fighter. But there was no prize to be had from taunting Adam Tyler.

'I couldn't let you guys go on for a second longer or I would have had to put out a fire.' He slapped Adam on the back, then approached Cara with his hand outstretched. 'You must be Cara. I'm Chris Geyer.'

'Hi, Chris,' she said, pumping his hand. 'I'm your stylist for the duration of the show.'

'Fantastic! I'm colour-blind and fashion unconscious so my life will be in your hands. Though watching you handle my bodyguard here is such a treat, even if you had no function I would ask to keep you on for that reason alone.'

She flicked a glance to Adam, who had relaxed enough to lean against the back of the couch, watching them.

'Aside from that, you just saved me from a pack of monsters in the other room,' Chris continued, rubbing at his chest. 'I just had my chest hair waxed to prepare me for the microphone I'll be wearing. I didn't plan on torture being part of the deal.'

'So why did you let Adam tag along?'

'Ooh! She got you there again, buddy. This one's sharp. We'll have to be quick around her.'

Cara adored Chris in a heartbeat. He was a teddy bear. With his sandy hair, his sightly pink cheeks, his not-so-hard body, his slightly rumpled suit, he would be a dream. A nice guy who would take to her plans like a duck to water. Whereas she knew that in the same position Adam would fight her tooth and nail. Though she also knew Adam would never put himself in the same position. He was the type of guy who kept his heart for pumping blood and nothing else. Just as she did herself.

Maybe that was why she felt so strange around him— they were like two north poles clashing and repelling over and over again. Whereas Chris was a definite south pole, easily compatible with both of them.

Adam watched over Chris like a hawk and Chris seemed to take it with good humour and the occasional roll of the eyes. She could sense the camaraderie between the two in an instant.

'So, Chris,' Cara said with a decisive clap of her hands. 'Let's go shopping.'

'Rightio,' Chris said. 'I'll just grab my key card thingy…'

Adam stood and held the key card up, showcasing the fact nobody was going anywhere without him.

'Great,' Chris said. 'Let's go.'

'Is he coming too?' Cara asked over her shoulder, loud enough for Adam to catch the words.

'It looks that way.'

She leaned into Chris and whispered rather loudly, 'Is there some way you can get him to lighten up? Otherwise it will be a long day.'

Chris whispered loudly back, 'Tell him our stock price has hit an all-time high. That ought to do it.'

'Your stock prices have hit an all-time high,' she threw over her shoulder, but Adam didn't even flinch. At the door to the room, Cara turned and faced him down. 'Just don't get in my way, OK? I'm the best at what I do and if you want your friend here to be the best that he can be, you'll need me on his side.'

Adam just stood there. And she found herself faltering under his steely glare. She fought the urge to bite her lip, which was a bad habit and a dead give-away when nerves hit.

Finally he spoke. 'I'm not planning on fighting any professional decision you might have to make. Put the guy in head-to-toe pink if that's your bag. But I am here to stay, sweetheart. So get used to it.'

Adam watched as she fought to contain herself. He could see the strain building within her: the quickening of her breath, the flare of her dazzling green eyes, and the shoulders squaring back. She was itching to deck him. He was shocked to find himself preparing to block a swinging fist.

She was like a firecracker and he knew it took very little to light her fuse. She certainly had some temper lurking just below the surface and he was pretty sure that something about him brought it out in her. Though it was probably nothing more than the fact that he pushed buttons for a living and did it in his day-to-day life without even meaning to.

Then from nowhere, with a heck of an effort, she collected herself, rolling her shoulders and physically slowing her breaths. Then she licked her lips, drawing his rapt attention to her shapely mouth, which was withdrawn from his sight all too soon as she spun away from him and headed out the door.

Chris shot him a big grin. 'She's a keeper.'

Adam shut the door behind them, pocketing the key card. 'We'll see,' he said, finding the very idea a dangerously appealing one.

When Adam realised it was going to be a day of barbers, beauticians and boutiques, spent under the watchful blinking red eye of a camera crew, he was ready to throw himself from the moving car. The only thing that kept him along for the ride was the fact that he knew Cara was wait-

ing for that exact reaction. She was waiting for the com-
plaints. She was longing for them. She all but begged for
them.

During Chris's manicure, her expression all innocence,
Cara offered Adam the chance to join Chris, to make his
friend feel more comfortable. Adam almost agreed, if only
to wipe that cheeky smile from her face. Though when he
turned down the invitation she sent him a saucy shrug and
joined Chris herself. The movement was rattling enough to
have him keep his mouth decidedly shut for the rest of the
day.

The women he knew didn't rattle him as this one did.
They were blissfully predictable. Yet he couldn't predict a
step Cara would make from one moment to the next. It was
disconcerting to say the least.

Later, when Cara had been choosing some appropriate
underwear for Chris to put on under some fairly fitted trousers, one of the crew made a comment about Cara's known
predilection for white cotton. News travelled fast in a small
community and Cara's grand entrance the night before must
have done the rounds and back again.

The whole room froze, waiting for Cara to fade away
into embarrassment or fly into bossy hysterics, either of
which would have been understandable. But she merely
turned, hand on hip, pierced the boom operator with a
steely glance, and said: 'Well, now you bring that up, since
you've all seen mine, I think it's only fair I see yours too.'

Then she took one quick step his way as though she was
about to chase him about the room with the intent to 'de-
brief' him. The boom operator flinched, his eyes wild with
panic, and that was all it took. The crew lost it, erupting
into loud fits of laughter that kept up for the rest of the
day. Suddenly he was the one under the microscope. He

was the one they would talk about at dinner. And Cara was instantly one of the gang.

Adam could have watched her work all day. In fact he quite happily did, even though the whole point of him being there was to keep Chris from the clutches of an unknown woman, and the last thing he needed to be doing was setting a bad example by obviously favouring one himself. But favour her he did. More and more every moment he was with her.

There was just something about her. Something in the way she managed to keep five guys doing her bidding without raising her voice. Something in the way she took care to keep Chris smiling all day. Something in the way her green gaze skimmed his way when she thought he wasn't watching.

So somehow it wasn't the most exasperating day of his life. Somehow with her impudent smiles and her teasing and her vivacious attitude, Cara made the whole day fly.

They hopped back into the limo a few hours later in good spirits.

'How are you holding up?' Chris asked and Adam glared him down. 'Don't look at me like that. I have never seen you look so morbid. You look like somebody died.'

'My friend Chris the man has gone. He has been replaced with Chris the dandy.'

'Anything for my little Cara,' Chris gushed. He took a hold of her face, squishing her cheeks between fingers and thumb, and remarkably she took the abuse. 'You just can't say no to this sweet face. You, who can charm anybody when you set your mind to it, were totally outclassed by this little lady today. If only we could headhunt her.'

'To do what?' Adam asked, his gaze lingering on the lady in question, who was hooking one foot beneath her in her seat, her companionable grin settled entirely upon Chris.

'Whatever she wanted.'

'This is plenty for me to handle just now, thanks,' the lady in question said.

'Have you worked for Jeff before?'

'Nope. First time for me too. But so far I like it and so far he likes me and I would like to keep it that way.'

'And by that you mean…?'

'They have enough faith in me to know that my work will be perfect. But that doesn't mean they can't sack me for any other reason they choose.'

'That's pretty tough.'

'Mmm. As I have been told, this is a tough business.' She waggled a finger at Chris. 'So be good. Don't cause me any trouble.'

Adam found her playful nature seriously attractive. Who was he kidding? Her porcelain skin, her long legs, her curling hair the colour of butterscotch, her cat's eyes, her luscious mouth, all were seriously attractive. She was a tough little chicken with confidence to spare, but her tendency towards the accident-prone seemed to bring out a strangely protective urge in him. She had him on constant alert, ready to whip out a steadying hand in case she stumbled.

All up she was a total mantrap and he was pretty certain she had no idea.

'So that's it for today?' Chris asked.

'Yep,' the mantrap said, mid yawn, her arms reaching across the expanse of the car as she stretched her whole body. Adam couldn't have dragged his eyes away if a gaggle of buxom blondes had sauntered by the car. 'And back to the hotel we go to prepare you for tonight. Are you excited?'

'I think so.'

Adam heard the uncertainty and his attention reverted back to exactly where it should have remained. On his friend. He pounced. 'It's not too late to turn back, mate. We can turn the car around, give those nice people back their fancy clothes, pay the hotel bill ourselves, and leave.'

'And why would you do that?' Cara asked, now fully alert, her smiles fading fast.

'Adam here thinks I am making a big mistake.'

'And what do you think?' Cara asked Chris. 'Are you ready to go ahead with this?'

'What do you care?' Adam asked.

The look Cara shot him was pure venom. The atmosphere in the car had gone from faintly prickly to toxic in an instant. It seemed those cat's eyes came with a matching set of claws. The faint sense of protective affection that he had been deluding himself he had been feeling throughout the day happily burst into a million imperceptible fragments.

'I care about what *your friend* wants. Chris?'

Chris nodded. 'Sure I'm nervous, but this is what I want.'

Cara turned back to Adam. 'So if you badger Chris into giving in now, that would mean he doesn't get what he wants. Is that what *you* really want?'

Adam clenched his teeth so hard his head hurt. And there he had been, feeling so clever that he knew how to push *her* buttons. 'No. It's not,' he admitted.

'Fabulous. Case closed. So let's do this thing and do it as best we can so that it works out for all of us.'

Cara shot a hand out the window and banged it twice on the roof. The driver got the message and took off back to the hotel.

Once there, Cara picked out Chris's clothes for the night, her movements so jerky Adam knew she was still none too happy with him.

'So what are you wearing, tonight?' she asked and, though she wasn't looking his way, Adam knew by the stern timbre of her voice she was talking to him.

'This, I guess.'

She shot him a look. Down and up, her glance travelled. Once it reached his face his whole body felt bombarded by her professional glance. If she had run a hand the length of the fabrics he wore, he would not have felt any less affected.

'I thought as much,' she said with a sigh and he knew that, whatever had been holding her at bay, he had been let off the hook. His relief was measurable. Substantial. Physical. Unforeseen.

She reached over and picked out one of the suit bags and all but threw it at him. He collected it in two hands. 'Adam Tux', written in large, strong handwriting on a white slip of paper, was safety-pinned to the outside of the bag.

'You got this for me?' he asked, feeling three steps behind her all the way.

'Mmm,' she said, with several pins poking out of her mouth. 'I heard the whole crew are getting dressed up tonight as well, to help get into the spirit of the thing, so I thought you might need it. Though after your little rebellion in the car I almost decided not to give it to you.'

She glanced his way from beneath lowered lashes and shot him a self-deprecating smile. Whoa. It rendered him speechless. He was never speechless. Sure, he wasn't a guy who talked people's ears off, but that was a cultivated mannerism created to get exactly what he needed from any conversation. He usually had plenty he could say on any given subject, he simply chose to listen instead. But on this occasion he was completely at a loss for words.

'Maybe after this you'll try to cut me some slack.' She

winked. Just once. And he felt it travel the room and lie upon his cheek like a feather-light kiss.

He took that as his cue to get the hell out of there. Without another word he took his tux, and his bafflement, and went to his suite to change. And to roll his incompetent tongue back into his mouth.

CHAPTER FIVE

THAT night, on the romantic, candlelit balcony of the Ivy Hotel ballroom, Chris set out to meet the woman he was going to marry, while Cara moved behind the scenes inside the ballroom proper in surroundings not nearly so romantic. Champagne glass in one hand, she used the other to hike up the heavy skirt of her slinky black dress so that she could better negotiate the light stands, cameras, and trailing cables stuck to the floor with heavy black gaffer tape.

She found Adam set up on a director's chair, which afforded a good view through the equipment to the scene outside. Despite the niggling tension she still felt licking between them, once the cameras began to roll she gravitated Adam's way.

'My stomach is curling as though I'm the one about to go out there,' she said, pulling up a chair.

Adam didn't even give her a glance, his focus was so fully on his friend. His whole body was clenched. He was like an explosion waiting to happen.

But it wasn't fair to say it was all him. She had been just as wound up earlier in the limo. At the talk of Chris pulling out of the show, the brick of fear inside her chest, which had been absent all day, had come back with a vengeance, so heavy it had threatened to pin her to the seat of the car.

The two of them were making their way through each day with the weight of the world on their shoulders and if she had to be around this sort of volatile energy for a fortnight, the finesse it would take to navigate him would eat her up inside.

She tried to get through to him again. 'Nerve-racking, isn't it?'

Nothing.

So she reached out a hand and placed it on his knee. He flinched so violently, she flinched in tandem. She could feel the tension radiating from him in waves. But what she saw in his deep blue eyes gave her pause. He wasn't being fractious. This wasn't some sort of manly power play. He was suffering.

She collected herself and placed her hand once more upon his knee. 'Are you OK?'

'You don't know him,' Adam said, his voice low and far away. 'He's too kind-hearted. Those women will eat him alive.'

She looked from him to Chris. Adam the confirmed bachelor, the playboy, the man about town, watching over his friend, the slightly younger, the sweeter, the less well travelled. They had made jokes earlier about Adam acting as Chris's bodyguard, but suddenly Cara knew it was no joke. For some reason, Adam felt he had to be there to protect his friend.

But why? As Cara saw it, the women, to a one, seemed to be even more nervous than Chris. She spied one other familiar face among them.

Well, what do you know? she thought. It was Maggie, the girl who had not been able to work her key card that morning. She was all dolled up in a pretty pink dress, her blonde tresses flowing straight and long past her shoulder blades. And Cara knew that if she was one to go by, the producers had picked good people. That girl would more likely build a campfire on the floor of her room than eat *anyone* alive.

'Give them a chance,' Cara said. 'If I think he's being taken advantage of, I will fight for him alongside you, OK?'

His gaze narrowed and she felt it focus on nothing but her. It was enough to sap her breath away.

'Don't play me, Cara.'

Her fluttery hand shot to her chest. 'I'm not. Seriously. I wouldn't even dare try. True, I barely know Chris, but I like him. And it's simply not in me to see someone like that be crushed.'

He nodded, slowly. Once. Twice. A deep breath filled his chest then released on a ragged sigh. Something in what she had said had hit the right note. His mouth kicked up at the corner. 'Allies.'

Her stomach clenched at that one small movement of his lips. He could be devastating when he chose to turn on the charm. But she had come into this conversation with one goal in mind, to make peace, and it seemed she had achieved her objective.

Cara held out a pinkie finger. 'Allies.'

Adam stared vacantly at her finger. Cara had to reach over, take his hand, and link his pinkie with hers. His hand warmed hers for a moment before the link was broken. The truce had been made. And too late Cara wondered if she had just made a pact with the devil and what sort of payment she would have to lay down to keep the peace with such a man.

'So are you taking notes?' she asked, lightening the loaded mood. 'So you can have your own show after this one?'

Adam laughed, the sound rumbling in his large chest. 'You got me. I'm pining to be out there myself.'

'Well, you're dressed the part, at least. And you do look pretty damn good in your tux if I do say so myself.'

He looked more than good. He looked absolutely edible.

Adam ran a hand down his white tie, but his eyes didn't leave hers. 'It's a perfect fit.'

Cara did her best not to blush, as beneath his words she heard him wonder how she had picked his measurements so well. 'It's my job, Adam,' she said. 'Don't get any ideas.'

His smile told her he was reserving judgment on her answer and she knew he had every right to. There would be plenty of women who could draw him from memory. He had that sort of magnetism that one could not help but stare if one had the chance.

'Or maybe you're not really planning to have your own show, maybe you are just here to ogle all the pretty girls,' Cara said, flicking a glance at the lovely ladies in evening dress fawning over his smiling friend.

He gave her a small grin, his eyes mercifully leaving her to rake over the other women before them.

But it wasn't long before his gaze drifted back to where it truly preferred to be, on by far the most beguiling woman in the room.

One minute she was sophisticated, with her dazzling red shoes and her portfolio, just the sort of woman he would happily spend a Saturday night seducing. The next minute she was the girl next door in her soft denim cut-offs and unbrushed curls, just the sort of *ingénue* he spent his waking hours avoiding.

Now tonight, with a dash of something dark about her eyes and gloss on her lips making them look as though she had eaten too many strawberries, she looked like sex on two legs and just the sort of woman who would surely be wearing something other than white cotton briefs beneath her clingy black dress.

Whereas he knew he had a Masters in the poker face, every thought flickered across her green eyes. Every blink told a story. Every twitch of her cheek said she had something to say. And if she nibbled at that full lower lip of hers a moment longer he would have to find out for himself how it tasted.

He knew it would be sweet. The longer he watched her nibble, the sweeter the thought became. He dragged his eyes back to face the same way as the cameras, but it was all he could do to concentrate on Chris.

After a couple more hours, day one of *The Billionaire Bachelor* shoot was over. The girls were herded out a back door while Chris trudged through the maze of cables and cameras to flop into a seat next to Adam.

'You looked great out there,' Cara said.

'Thank God that's over, hey?' Adam suggested.

Chris didn't move, his head flung back, his eyes closed. Finally he shook his head, slowly, back and forth. 'I could have stayed out there for the rest of my life.'

Cara felt Adam's whole body tense in response. His cheek muscles clenched and his knuckles showed white on his large tanned hands. If she had brought him to an uneasy peace earlier, the caged tiger was back with a vengeance.

Chris opened his eyes and Cara's breath caught in her throat. He was positively glowing.

'They were all amazing. Lovely. Sweet. Beautiful. I don't know what I ever did to deserve this. It's going to work. I can feel it in my bones. Within that group of women is the woman I am going to marry.'

If Adam was tense before, by that stage he had practically turned to stone.

'Was there any one in particular who caught your fancy?' Cara asked, trying to keep the spirit lively.

'Maybe. Possibly.' Chris thought about it, then his neck

began to turn pink. He sat up and shook his head. 'But it's too early to know.'

He seemed to just notice Adam, and Chris's expression went from delighted to grim in an instant. 'Adam, just relax.'

Cara blinked. She had not heard Chris so bothered before.

'Remember, they have no idea who I am. None of them know the title of the show is *The Billionaire Bachelor*. I am just Chris. There is no way they are in this for anything other than finding someone to love, just like I am.'

Adam laughed, or as much as it could be a laugh considering he looked fit to burst.

'You are going to have to get over this, mate,' Chris insisted. 'I'm here. I am doing this. And no matter your reservations and your history with relationships, you are going to have to suck it up and support me. Because I seriously can't do this without your cooperation.'

Cara could see that Adam was dealing with some pretty heavy emotions. There was a war going on within him so distressing even *he* couldn't keep it under wraps. He breathed deeply through his nostrils, stretched out his fingers and relaxed his shoulders. These were movements she knew all too well herself. The reeling back of one's temper, of one's true feelings in order to keep the peace. She wondered what it was about his 'history with relationships' that had him so heated.

Whatever else, she could see how much he cared for Chris. And for whatever reason he was torn between taking him by the ear and pulling him out of the hotel and all the way home, and letting him be. Adam was keenly afraid that Chris might fall for one of these women. Whereas Cara and every woman who would watch the show would hope for nothing less for sweet, fluffy Chris, it was the last thing in the world Adam wanted for him. And it was more than just wanting his friend to remain free and easy.

'So come on, Adam,' Chris continued. 'I need to know, here and now, that, despite your reservations, you will stick by me whatever decision I might make.'

Ever the diplomat, Cara ached to get between them and make it all OK. To do a little dance. Sing a little song. Anything to draw attention away from the tension. But she sensed that this time she wasn't needed. There was enough history, enough understanding between these two they could work it out and it wouldn't end in cold shoulders.

Adam finally dug deep enough to find what he was looking for. 'Fine. You know my feelings—'

'Unfortunately I do.'

'But no matter what you decide to do, I'm with you. Why else do you think I'm here?'

'To rouse at me?'

'To be your second. To be your shoulder.'

Cara wondered if the guys even remembered she was there. But she was used to sinking into the background while moments of high emotion rolled on by. She always felt it was better to live on an even plane—knock off the edges both high and low, and she would be much more content.

Chris gave him a lopsided grin. 'So you are.' He shook his head. 'Sorry, mate. I guess my head is just too full to take it all in. I'm used to figures and measurements, and not those concerning the ladies. We're all good?'

'We're all good.'

The two men stood and, where she would have expected shaking of hands, they hugged. Actually honest to goodness hugged. And she wondered again on the history that had brought them together. Such true friendship. A relationship built on rock.

Though she had spent her life rejecting the notion, for the first time in a long while she ached to be in the middle of the action. She yearned to reach out and take a little of that emotion before it rolled on by and out of her life for ever.

The next day, since the girls were piled into a couple of minibuses and taken to the local mall for their day of shopping and pampering, all under the watchful eye of a three-man location camera crew, everyone else had the day off.

But after the emotional invigoration of the night before, Cara could not stand being alone in her room. After an hour of channel flicking and floor pacing she was about to pick up the phone, and call Jeff and see if he wanted a game of cards, I-spy, whatever, when her room phone rang. She leapt across the bed to grab it.

'Good morning, Cara,' Adam's low voice coursed down the phone line.

'Good morning, Adam.' She sat down, her knees simply unable to hold her up. It was the voice, nothing else. He just had that type of voice that would kick at something deep inside any woman. She had been able to think of little else since the emotional display the night before. Zinging as if she had downed a carafe of coffee all on her own, she had nibbled away the fingernails on her left hand the night before in penance for imagining herself wrapped in Adam's arms in Chris's place.

'How does a day of fresh air and sunshine grab you?' he asked.

With him? Unexpectedly that grabbed her in all the right places.

'Don't tease me like that,' she said.

She couldn't give him an outright *no way* as that would

only mean spending a day alone, nibbling away the finger-nails on her right hand.

'This is no tease, I assure you,' he said, his voice typically unhurried. It was almost hypnotic.

Cara lay back on the bed and cradled the phone under her ear. 'So what did you have in mind?'

'We have been given permission from the powers that be to have a day outdoors.'

'But I thought the idea was to keep us out of the light so that we don't remember what day it is, what time of day, what our names are, where we really live…'

Adam's soft laughter reverberated down the line and Cara was glad she was lying down. The mellow sound turned her whole body to jelly.

'We will be under strict supervision, of course,' he assured her.

'Sounds kinky.'

Cara slapped her hand across her forehead. Where had that come from? She waited for his reply and she had to endure several moments of humiliated silence before it came.

'Wear comfortable clothes and sneakers and meet me downstairs in fifteen minutes.'

'What for?' Cara asked, but Adam had already rung off.

She stared at the phone for a moment before her adrenalin kicked in. Tearing her clothes off as she went, she ran into her closet to find her most comfortable clothes and her sneakers, her mind reeling with ideas of what Adam could have had in mind.

Outdoors. Supervised.

Whatever it was she was giddy with excitement, and was out the door in ten minutes flat, lathered in sunscreen, wide-brimmed hat on her head, more excited than she was prepared to admit.

*   *   *

As it turned out she was to spend the day with Adam, the majority of the television crew and half the staff from the hotel for a game of baseball in the private park next door to a suburban hotel owned by the same chain.

Cara couldn't play baseball to save her life. It took her enough daily effort to navigate high heels without having to master the necessary coordination to play a team sport. The best she could hope for was that she wouldn't trip over her laces and land face down in the dirt. But here she was, in her cut-off jeans, sleeveless top and sneakers, her wide-brimmed hat long since laid aside to accommodate the blue cap that showed her up as a being on the Blue TV Team as opposed to the Red Hotel Team. It was to be a battle to the death.

She stood out in right field, bent at the waist, hands on knees, legs shoulder-width apart, waiting for someone to hit the ball her way so she could make the split-second decision to duck and squeal, or have a go and fumble it in front of everyone. Hmm. Nail biting suddenly seemed like a rather pleasant way to spend a day.

'How you going, Cara?' Chris called out from second base.

She gave him a hearty salute and by his ringing laughter she figured he had guessed just how she was going.

Cara turned her attention back to the game at hand. She punched her glove a couple of times as she had seen the players on television do, then hunched over, resting her hands on her knees, preparing herself for whatever came her way.

Adam, the pitcher for their team, looking resplendent in cut-off track pants and a loose-fitting T-shirt, lazily threw the ball into the air and caught it in his free hand as he talked behind his glove with his catcher, Mickey the boom mike operator.

Then he sidled back onto the mound, his long, loping strides catching at Cara. He was so effortlessly sexy that it created an ache deep in her stomach. Who knew that beneath those layered suits there was a body like the one working before her? The back of his shirt was stuck to his broad torso. He had a great pair of legs, strong, muscled and tanned, and in his loose shorts he gave her a prime view of the best masculine behind she had ever set eyes on. And she had seen some hunks. Most men she styled were models or actors, and kept themselves fit through many waking hours spent at the gym. But nevertheless this guy was a notch above. He was broad, and strong, and tall and had a simply pinchable behind. And she had no doubt it was all natural.

As he prepared to pitch, Cara saw that his beautiful hands came with a matching pair of beautiful arms. They were sinewy, bronzed and shaped like those of a swimmer. Those gorgeous arms stretched and twisted and threw the ball with such amazing power and grace it slammed over the home plate with ease and precision.

'Cara, it's yours, babe,' Chris called out.

Cara stood up straight, shielding her eyes with her hand, to find the ball was bouncing raggedly across the ground her way. She sensed her team all turning, facing her as the batter rounded first base and kept on going to second.

She flicked a momentary glance at Adam and knew she shouldn't have. If the view from the back was something, the view from the front with his shirt stuck to his muscular chest, his dark, damp hair curling about his face, his mouth open to rake in great dragging breaths, his eyes bright from exercise, his chest rising and falling… It was too beautiful to believe.

Cataloguing his features this way was suddenly no professional habit. This had nothing to do with any sort of professional survival mechanism. She was fast becoming bewitched by the guy.

Clearing her throat, she dragged her gaze away and waited for the ball. It bounced wildly at the final moment but she caught it, awkwardly, with her forearms.

'Straight to me!' Chris called.

Cara shuffled it into her hands and threw with all her might, meaning the ball took two bounces to reach him at second base. But reach him it did, just before the batter rounded it into second. He was tagged. Third man out. First innings; the Red Hotel Team nil.

Cara couldn't believe it. She leapt into the air and let out a great whoop, then ran infield to meet up with her team who were all jogging to the bench ready to bat.

Adam waited on the mound until she had reached him, his eyes on her, all but ignoring the pats on the back he received from his passing team mates.

Cara slowed to a walk and they headed off the field together.

'Well done, Ms Marlowe.'

'Please. We were lucky it came straight to me.'

'I kind of thought you might be more mindful of your new manicure.'

Cara blinked. 'Did you now? Well, that shows how little you know about me, doesn't it, Mr Tyler? Though I am a girl who likes a good manicure, I am a girl who likes winning more.' Point made, she quickened her pace until she strode away from him.

Adam was getting used to watching her walk away. Her head was held high. Her short curly pony-tail bounced as she walked. She swayed almost saucily. But he knew she was no sportswoman. Her perfectly white sneakers had been the initial give-away.

His gaze travelled up from her sneakers. Up long, smooth legs, over her denim-clad hips, over her dainty waist, and a back held ramrod straight just for his benefit. She was a spitfire, this one. Too damn impudent for her own good. And she was dealing with someone who could give as good as he got in that department. Didn't she realise that?

He kind of liked the fact that maybe she did realise it, yet it didn't stop her for a second.

As she reached the bench she sat down with a fresh bottle of water and glanced back at him from beneath her cap. Her green eyes shot fire. And he was suddenly thankful she was on his team. In her cute little outfit, meant more for a leisurely picnic than a rough and tumble game, she was distracting enough being on the same team. She would be one heck of a troublesome opponent.

Who was he kidding? She had been one heck of a troublesome opponent from the moment she'd got the job. But also the most fun he'd had being at cross purposes with a woman.

Though there was a seat right next to her, he took a space at the other end of the bench and he could still feel the daggers she was shooting at him with her eyes. It made him smile.

Chris was up first.

'Pitch to him carefully, mate,' Jeff called out to the hotel team's pitcher. 'If he gets a black eye I'll sue you and your hotel for all you're worth.'

The pitcher lowered his ball, his eyes growing wide.

Jeff leant over to Adam and through his teeth said, 'They're toast!'

The pitcher all but threw underarm and Chris hit an easy double. Then a grinning Jeff followed with a single.

Adam was third man up. He shot a look Cara's way as

he walked to home plate but she was steadfastly looking anywhere but at him. His smile grew bigger.

Standing at the mound, he swung his bat several times to warm his shoulders. He then positioned himself ready for the pitch. He was kind of showing off and he knew exactly who for: a girl who admitted she liked to win. But they *were* on the same team so why play down his prowess? Why not help her get her wish? Adam set himself up to hit the hell out of the ball. The pitcher pitched. Adam swung. And he missed.

'Come on, Adam,' Jeff called out from first base. 'Don't sweat it. Swing and hit, buddy. Swing and hit.'

Adam felt his cheeks warm and he knew it wasn't the weak spring sunshine that was doing it.

He could all but sense Cara smirking at his back.

He couldn't help himself. He had to see it for himself. But when he flicked a glance over his shoulder he found she wasn't smirking: she was leaning forward, her elbows resting on her knees, her chin resting on her fingers, which she had positioned as a steeple. Her cheeks looked as warm as his felt.

And her eyes were not on his face, but lower. The woman had been checking out his butt! She blinked several times, then her gaze finally locked with his and she all but fell off her seat when she found he was watching her.

He turned away. Readied himself for the pitch. Swung. And missed. But it was not pride that stopped him that time, but the fact that his thoughts were anywhere but on the game. They were on the pink cheeks and bright, telling eyes of the compelling woman sitting behind him, and wondering where those telling eyes were focussed at that moment. He was used to women eyeing him up as if he were a prime rib, but this was different. Perhaps because it was unexpected. She'd given his ego enough of a bashing he had thought she was immune to his attractions. And the fact that she was not immune shook him up.

Adam squared his shoulders and focussed his attention on the game.

The pitcher smiled as he lined up. Smiled! As though Adam were some sort of lightweight and it was only a matter of time before he beat him.

Adam smiled back. *Come on, kid,* he thought. *Give me all you've got.*

The kid pitched. Adam swung. And connected. It was only a single. But he made it to first base with tremendous relief.

The next two batsmen were caught out. But the bases were still loaded.

Cara was up next. She stood. She picked up a bat between two fingers and Adam knew she had never held a baseball bat in her life.

She stood at home base and swung the bat in much the same way he had, and he knew she had no idea why she was doing it. It was adorable. Then she set her feet apart, lifted the bat, turned to face the pitcher and swallowed hard.

'Come on, Cara,' Chris called out. 'Easy does it.'

Jeff called out, clapping. 'Whack it for all you're worth.'

Adam could see her considering. Easy does it, or whack it for all she was worth. And this to a girl who was still unsure she was holding the correct end of the bat.

'Cara,' Adam called out and saw her eyes swing wildly his way. 'If you manage to even hit the ball I'll shout you a new manicure.'

Her mouth dropped open. Then her eyes narrowed, and she wiggled her bottom and adjusted her stance. Her determination was palpable.

The pitcher pitched and Cara's eyes clamped tight shut

as she whacked the ball with every ounce of strength in her slender arms. The ball shot between the pitcher and the short stop and bounced past second base. Jeff jumped to let it between his legs and then he took off.

Adam watched as Cara opened her eyes, shock that she had hit the ball evident in her wide eyes.

'Cara, run!' Adam called out. She nodded then ran, the bat still in her hot little hand. Adam took off, his gaze swinging back to home plate to see that Chris had made it home.

The centre fielder misfielded so Jeff was able to follow Chris home. Adam rounded it towards third, jogging backwards the last few steps as the fielder picked up the ball. He stopped, turned, and saw Cara had made it to first and had pressed on. She was running towards second, and the second baseman had taken up residence there, awaiting the incoming throw.

It was tight. As tight as a race could get. Cara looked up and he saw the moment she knew it was going to be tight. She put her head down and ran.

The noise from the Blue Team bench was deafening. The fielder threw the ball, the second baseman readied himself and Cara was within reach.

The ball curved through the air in a beautiful arc. Cara saw it coming and, mustering every ounce of determination, she tucked one knee beneath her and in an all encompassing swirl of dust, and a great echoing crack, took a magnificent slide into the base, taking out the fielder in the process until they ended up in a tangled pile of dirt and arms and legs.

CHAPTER SIX

EVERYONE rushed to second base, but Adam got there first. That crack had sounded too ominous for his liking. He slid to his knees, dragging the fielder from on top of Cara.

'Cara,' he called, his voice tearing from him painfully. He reached out to her but couldn't touch her, fearing he might hurt her. What if that crack had been one of her bones? Or, God forbid, her neck? 'Sweetheart, are you OK?'

Cara twisted about until she was on her knees herself. She was covered in dust from head to toe. Her cap had fallen off and bits of her hair had escaped from her pony-tail. Finally unable to stand it any longer Adam ran furious hands over her head feeling for lumps, blood, anything that might mean that she was badly hurt.

'Are you hurt?' he asked.

She winced and his whole body clenched as she reached beneath her and pulled out half her bat. Adam found a thankful laugh rising in his throat as he realised it had been the splintering bat, which she had carried with her the whole way, and not any bones that had broken.

Finding nothing else wrong, he grabbed her face between his hands and looked deep into her eyes, and the joy that spread through him when he saw her eyes were lively and focussed was not something he wished to dissect.

Then she looked up at him and spat a clump of grass from her mouth. 'Was I safe?'

'Excuse me?'

'Was I safe? Did I get here first?'

Adam looked over to the second baseman who was back on his feet. He held out his empty hands. 'Never even had the ball,' the guy admitted.

Adam ran one hand down Cara's face, his thumb wiping away a smear of dirt from her pale cheek. 'You were safe, Cara. Safe but now a total mess.'

She shrugged. 'I don't mind. I was promised a manicure so tomorrow I'll be fine.'

'You are one surprising lady, Ms Marlowe.'

She beamed at him. Her teeth showing perfect white from within her dusty face. 'I can live with that.'

After the third innings, they sat down for lunch, everyone grabbing what they wanted from an array of cold meats and salads laid out on a picnic table. Cara made herself a huge ham roll, then sat down on a patch of grass under a large gum tree.

'Do you mind if I join you?'

Cara squinted up into Adam's face. He was shrouded in sunlight, his face seeming dark and ominous in the over-bright sunshine.

'Of course not, Cap'n.'

Cara shuffled over so he had room on her patch of grass without them having to sit too close. Ever since he had caught her staring, she'd felt an awareness pulsating between them that she did not wish to encourage.

'Having fun?' she asked.

He took a bite of his roll and nodded.

'Thanks for today,' she said.

He shot her a quick salute.

'The crew all look like little boys in a toy store. The idea of fresh air and sunshine appeal a heck of a lot more than four walls and weekend television.'

He watched her without expression and nodded again.

That was all she could take.

'I don't get it. You are purported to be this great communicator. One-time Australian Businessman of the Year, who can change any person's mind with the use of nothing but his verbal skills. A man who can charm women out of their…inhibitions. Yet I can *still* barely get you to string two words together.'

Adam chewed, and chewed, and chewed, and then swallowed. 'I had a mouthful of food,' he finally said.

Cara was sure she heard a hint of cheekiness in his voice, but by the time she looked at him through narrowed eyes he had already tucked into his next mouthful. Since clenching her hands would only mean that the contents of her roll would end up on her lap, she had to settle for clenching her toes in her sneakers.

Cara took another mouthful herself and was careful to swallow just before he did.

'That has not been the reason in the past,' she persisted.

He continued to chew several times before swallowing his food. 'If all a question requires is a yes or a no answer, that's all you're going to get from me.'

'It's really frustrating.'

Adam laughed. 'OK, then. What would you like to talk about?'

Cara opened her mouth but had nothing in particular to say.

'Come on. You ask, I'll answer. This is your big chance to partake of my renowned ''verbal skills''.'

His last words came to her almost as a purr and Cara racked her brain for something to say but her mind was rendered blank. The longer she struggled, the bigger Adam's smile became, until slowly, slowly he raised his roll to his mouth as a sign that her time was running out.

'So why telecommunications?' she finally blurted, the relief she felt ridiculous.

But Adam, as promised, lowered his roll and talked.

'That was all Chris. We went to uni together. He was the studious guy with his head always in a pile of books. I was the party guy at uni, my majors being girls and beer.'

Cara felt a funny kick in her stomach. It felt a heck of a lot like a jealous stab, which was insane. She continued eating while he talked in case it was merely hunger making her tummy feel so tight.

'But we were always friendly,' Adam continued. 'He even got me my first real job, selling mobile phones and accessories in his uncle's store on nights and weekends.'

She couldn't quite picture him working in a shopping centre hocking mobile-phone contracts to innocent passers-by. Though she had the feeling that if he took it upon himself to try, he could do it without breaking a sweat. Any woman caught in that resolute blue gaze would be locked in until he chose to let her loose.

But as far as she could tell he had chosen to let them loose every time thus far. At that thought, her tummy problems eased considerably.

'My way through college was already covered so I didn't need the job, but Chris insisted that it would be good for me, and he was right. Unless you have worked your butt off for under ten dollars an hour, there is no way you can create sellable products for people in exactly that socio-economic bracket.'

'Born with a silver spoon in your mouth?' Cara asked, already knowing the answer but aware of a need to know how he felt about the fact.

'Diamond-encrusted platinum, actually,' he said with a wry smile. 'And you?'

'A wooden spoon, I'm afraid.' *And at least one foot.*

Adam blinked, sudden humour lurking deep beneath his dark blue eyes. 'And who is your mobile phone carrier?' he asked.

'You guessed it. Revolution Wireless,' Cara admitted.

'You are my bread and butter,' he said with a charming smile.

And the smile did it. Though he was just highlighting the fact that she was struggling and he was stratospherically wealthy because of people like her, his smile still made her toes unclench and her tummy flip over on itself. Her tummy needed a good talking to!

Cara managed to stop herself from snapping at him that she already had one of his bloody phones and he didn't need to sweet-talk her into making him more money. But she did say, 'I'll have you know I earn more than ten dollars an hour, buddy.'

He held up his hands in submission, his charming smile breaking into outright laughter. 'And I'm sure you're worth every cent.'

Cara could not help but smile either. So he was rich. She wasn't. There was no point in arguing the fact. It was empirical. Unchangeable. And such a nasty thing to get worked up over. She of all people should remember that.

'One day after work,' Adam continued, 'Chris approached me. He told me he had a business plan and only with the two of us working together could it be achieved. And I was hooked.'

'What was his plan?'

Adam smiled. 'It was fairly detailed and I dozed off through half of it, but when he hit the point about becoming a millionaire on my own by the age of twenty-five, I shut up and listened. He had me. He says that I'm the salesman of the crew, but he sure knew what would hook me that day.'

Abba had it figured out long ago. 'Money, money, money'—everything came down to money. But who was she to argue? The thought of living comfortably took up most of her waking moments, so why shouldn't Adam be the same? Her dad always said money made the world go around and he was right. Even if on the flipside it could turn people against each other, and make them bitter and cynical into the bargain.

Cara bit into her roll to show that the conversation was over. She could feel Adam watching her but she'd said and heard enough to think maybe she shouldn't have demanded so much information from him in the first place.

They sat for several long moments in conjoined silence. Keeping her eyes straight ahead, Cara tried hard to focus on watching the sunshine send dappled shadows through the leaves of the big old gum tree and listening to the crickets singing in the nearby underbrush.

Then finally Adam spoke. 'Was that what you were after?'

Cara sent him a sideways glance accompanied by a hasty nod. But he wasn't finished.

'Or were you hoping I might try to charm *you* out of *your* inhibitions?'

Cara swallowed too fast, and coughed and spluttered in response. She shot to her feet as gracefully as she could, her eyes searching wildly for an escape route.

'Looks like the game's about to begin again. So…see you there.'

And then she strode away as fast as her sneakers would carry her.

The rest of the game went pretty much the same. Though the hotel guys made a brief comeback in the next-to-last innings, the TV Team won easily: ten runs to three.

Everyone hopped back in the hotel bus in high spirits. Cara was the last one inside and the only spare seat was across the aisle from Adam.

She gave him a short smile before sitting down. Although she was well aware of every rise and fall of his chest, every flicker of his eyelids, every shuffle of his large frame in the small seat, she still got a fright when his hand landed upon her knee.

'You're bleeding,' he said.

She looked down at her calf where a trickle of dried blood was smeared. She watched in shocked silence as Adam rolled up the leg of her cut-off jeans to reveal a pretty nasty scrape on her knee. But Cara was less aware of that than of his hands creating a warm rush that reached deep within her stomach.

'Didn't you know you were hurt?' Adam asked, his brow furrowed in concern.

Cara shrugged. She was sore all over from that stupid proud slide of hers, and, though her knee had stung ever since, it was one of many bumps and bruises that would only look worse by the next day.

'Wait here,' he said before leaving her to walk up to the front of the bus to grab the first-aid kit from the driver.

When he returned, Cara held out her hands to take it but Adam ignored her. He sat down in his seat, his legs stretched out into the aisle so that he was facing her. He gently dragged her knee so that it was settled between his.

'Oh, no, you don't,' Cara insisted, all but scrambling onto her seat as far away as she could get. 'I can do this myself.'

Adam shot her a look from beneath his dark lashes that shut her up fast. It also caused the warmth in her stomach to spread to the rest of her body.

'You are not going anywhere near this scrape with those

filthy hands,' Adam insisted, going through the bits and bobs until he found some antiseptic, cotton wool and a bandage.

Cara hadn't really noticed how dirty she was. Compared with her just-as-dirty arms, her hands hadn't looked particularly bad, but, sitting in the clean air-conditioned bus, she suddenly realised how gritty she felt. Her hair was stuck to the back of her neck, her feet felt damp with sweat, and she could even taste dirt in her mouth. She must have looked frightful.

But then Adam touched her knee with a patch of antiseptic-covered gauze and she forgot all about how she must have looked as a sharp pain took the place of all other sensations, good or bad.

'Yowza!' she shouted.

Adam looked up, his spare hand moving to rest gently on her thigh.

'Did I hurt you? Am I too hard?'

He was doing the furrowed-brow thing again and she had to swallow to wet her dry throat. Besides which, his hand was still resting on her thigh. Gently. On her thigh, for goodness' sake! Pain gone. Good sensation back.

She shook her head. 'No,' she croaked. 'It's fine.'

Adam's brow smoothed out as he looked deep into her eyes. He didn't believe her for a second and she could see that he wanted to make sure she was not hurting in any way. She looked back, hoping beyond hope that he saw none of her deep awareness shining from her eyes. 'Really, Adam. It was just cold. That's all.'

He nodded shortly then went back to his job, which entailed running soft cotton pads lightly over her knee. Slowly. Softly. What was he doing being so tender? Adam was meant to be unsympathetic, gruff and unperturbed. Not delicate, and comforting, so much so that the sting was soon nothing compared with the sensation raging through her at his deft touch from his beautiful fingers. Those fingers that were as sure and as warm and as skilled as she had imagined.

This was bad. The last thing she needed was to find herself thinking such disturbing and ultimately distracting thoughts when she was meant to be focussed on her job. Maya had warned her to be good, but her imagination was being very, very naughty.

All the same Cara watched Adam's face as he went about his job. He was silent with concentration. Every fibre of his being was focussed totally on the task at hand. She had never met anyone who could focus so fully. Her mind was never settled. No matter which job she was on, she was thinking ahead to the next three. Yet this guy, with millions at stake in every conversation he had, could leave all that behind just so that her knee would be clean and germ-free.

He pulled out a bandage and wrapped it neatly across the scrape. Mission accomplished, his gaze travelled back to meet hers. There was a smile in his eyes. Simple pride at a job well done. What could she do but smile back?

'Thanks, Adam. That was very kind of you. Unnecessary, but kind.'

He rested both hands about her calf, encircling the width as he had encircled his baseball bat earlier, with familiarity and finesse.

'We can't have this leaving a scar,' he said. 'Your legs are too nice for that.'

She raised one eyebrow, careful not to let him see how his words and his touch were affecting her. 'Are you flirting with me, Adam Tyler?' she asked, trying to keep the conversation light.

His smile grew, kicking into a grin. 'What if I am?'

Now that was a question loaded with trouble and she had

been incredibly stupid to invite it. So it was up to her to bring it to a close.

'Then maybe you should stop.'

His smile stayed, but his hands began to move, slowly travelling down the length of her leg.

'All work and no play—'

'Means that Cara will take home pay.'

His hands stopped, meaning Cara's breathing could re-start.

Their gazes clashed. Held. Fought a battle of wills all on their own. Cara ached to look away but she knew she couldn't. This was no time to seem coy. No time to seem unsure. She did not want some sort of holiday fling with this guy—this guy with the sort of strong, sure hands that could take a woman's breath away. This job meant the world to her, and nothing and nobody was going to jeopardise that. No matter how unexpectedly considerate and unquestionably sexy and...

The bus suddenly slowed.

'We're home, guys!' Jeff called out and the crew groaned as one.

Cara and Adam still stared.

'But think of the hot shower and buffet dinner that awaits,' Jeff yelled, and the crew cheered as one.

Then finally Adam blinked. Slowly. But it was enough. His hands eased away, leaving a zinging trail of heat as they slipped off her leg. And as the crew tumbled down the aisle of the bus Cara was left to wonder if the strange, heady encounter had all been a heat-induced dream. Maybe she had concussion after all. Whatever she had, it made her feel hot and cold and breathless all at once.

That hot shower, followed by dinner *alone* in her room, sounded like just what the doctor ordered.

*   *   *

The next day, Cara spent the morning working hard following Chris and the girls around the glorious Melbourne Zoo. She primped, she preened, and she even helped out with the girls when she found the chance, anything to feel as though she was contributing as much as she possibly could. So by Sunday afternoon, happily tired from a hard day's work, she felt as if she had actually earned a little down time lazing by the pool.

After a quick refreshing dip, she was back in the shade of a large beach umbrella, lathered in sunscreen, damp hair tucked up into her wide-brimmed hat, and sheer white shirt covering her black bikini.

Lying on a sun lounger, she stared contentedly upwards, watching for long minutes as the small puffs of cotton wool clouds drifted across the wide expanse of beautiful blue Melbourne sky. The fat green leaves on the banana palms behind her rustled heavily in the warm spring breeze.

She mused over the fact that the night before was the first Saturday Night Cocktails get-together she had ever missed since the tradition began. While Kelly had been honeymooning, she and Gracie had kept up the tradition in her absence, meeting at Cara's for nights of cocktails and gossip. And the night before, tossing and turning in bed, she'd known if they had come together as usual she would have been the one asking for advice, not the one giving it. But by morning she was seriously glad the secrecy of the show had meant she'd had to forgo any meeting with Gracie.

How would she have explained her concerns, anyway?

'There's this guy. Don't know him well, or at all, really. Super rich. Dates models. Has eyes that I am sure can see right through me, and hands that make me blush every time I think of them. Glares at me more often than not but called me sweetheart when he thought I was hurt.'

No way. If she had said all of that Gracie would have raised one perfectly groomed eyebrow and told her to get a grip, or on the flipside would have goaded her incessantly and called her sweetheart in every conversation they had for a week.

Nope. Cara was seriously glad that, this weekend of all weekends, Saturday Night Cocktails had been postponed. Now she could rest easy that her disquiet had gone no further than her own sleepy head.

Instead Cara planned on enjoying her afternoon off spent with a book she had borrowed from the hotel library.

'Is this seat taken?' The deep, familiar voice that had invaded her sleepless night now invaded her happy alone thoughts.

She opened one eye to find Adam looking down upon her through a pair of dark sunglasses. 'What if I said it was?'

'Then I would say they should have left a towel upon the chair to bar it, else someone consider it fair game.'

Considering the provocative smile that kicked at the corner of his mouth, Cara felt the sudden urge to cover herself in a towel too. Their fleeting flirty conversations of the day before came back with such a rush she felt as if they were still mid-sentence—as though a whole day hadn't passed since they had last laid eyes on each other.

She wished she hadn't encouraged him to talk more in the first place. He seemed to have quite taken to the idea, and every second sentence that came out of his mouth seemed to be intended to charm her out of her indiscretions. She and her impatient ways.

Having had enough of him glaring down at her she fluttered a hand at the empty sun lounger beside her. 'It's all yours. I was just leaving anyway.'

As Cara made to sit up and gather her belongings Adam

rested a hand on her shoulder. She felt its warmth all the way to her curling bare toes.

'No, you weren't,' he drawled. 'Just stay, Cara. I promise I won't disturb you.'

Ha! He had no choice on that matter. That was the problem. But Cara did as she was told, sinking back against the chair more to shrink from his enclosed palm than anything else.

He dragged the white towel from across his shoulders and threw it down upon the lounger. It was only then that Cara realised he was wearing nothing but swim trunks. She looked away, hard though it was to drag her eyes from such a sight.

But when he ambled over to the water, her gaze was invariably drawn to him once more. He shook out his long limbs, the muscles in his back and arms clenching and stretching as he went. What a specimen. He was a supremely built man. Tall, sculptured, strong, tanned. Cara knew that beside him she would look like a scrawny, underfed, indoorsy waif. No wonder he was always photographed arm in arm with models, and Amazonian ones at that. Any other woman would be engulfed by his presence.

He dived in the pool with a sleek splash and it knocked Cara from her panting reverie. Now he was out of her eyesight, his presence only felt through the light slap of water as he swam lengths of the pool, Cara purposely lost herself within the pages of her book.

'I can't believe it,' Adam said half an hour later.

Cara lowered her book to squint at him. He was standing before her, dripping onto the pool tiles, his black swim trunks plastered to his lean hips, his torso sleek with water, his hair raked back and darkened from the pool water, his eyelashes clumped and spiky, his dark blue eyes bright and clear.

And for the life of her Cara could not remember what he had just said. 'I'm sorry?'

He pointed. 'That book. Where on earth did you find it?'

Aah. She had a good long look at the cover, which read, 'Unauthorised: Three Generations of Tylers'.

She grinned. 'Hotel library.'

'Meaning it was a book some discerning guest left behind in disgust,' Adam said, his voice deep with chagrin.

'Mmm. Makes sense to me.'

Adam raked a hand through his wet hair and flicked the gathered water droplets at her. She squealed, shielding herself with the hardcover.

'Why are you reading that trash?' he asked as he reached for his towel and dried himself down.

Cara half wished he wouldn't do that in front of her. But then she half wished he would do it in front of her for a good long time.

'Oh, I don't know. I was looking for something lightweight to read on my afternoon off.'

He stopped drying, swung the towel onto the sun lounger and lay his long frame upon it. His head turned her way, his deep blue eyes no longer clear, back to being dark and unfathomable. 'Lightweight, eh?' he said.

'Well, the subject matter is, of course, very heavy and important,' she said with a grin, 'but the manner in which it is presented is…lightweight to say the least.'

'Mmm,' he growled. 'So I have been told.'

'You haven't read it?'

'Hell, no.'

'Why not? It's a riot. Here, let me quote. This is from the chapter named: ''The Son and Heir''. That's you,' she qualified.

The smile Adam shot back was distinctly lacking in mirth.

'"*Stricken from an early age by his father's numerous nuptials and infamous infidelities, young Adam Tyler, son and heir, seemed intent not to follow in his father's large footsteps, choosing instead to date prolifically, not marry, and thus to keep his own self-made fortune intact. And yet the ladies in his life have been abundant and encumbered.*" See, I didn't make this stuff up about your infamy with buxom blondes.'

Cara looked up to find Adam staring at the sky, his jaw set tight. No wonder he was so protective of Chris, she thought. And of himself. His 'history with relationships' that Chris had once thrown at him was hardly littered with giggles and sunshine. Had his father's less-than-fine example numbed him to the possibility of enjoying a real relationship?

'Give me that,' Adam ordered, his hand suddenly shooting out to grab at the book. But Cara was quick off the mark. She shrugged out of his way, squirming and turning from his grabbing hand.

Adam sprang to his feet and, sensing failure, Cara did the same, rolling off the other side, her hat falling off her head and her air-dried curls tumbling from their makeshift constraint. They faced each other with her chair between them, their chests rising and falling in tandem, Cara with the book clutched tight to hers.

'Give it to me,' Adam ordered, his voice ominous.

'Or else what? You'll throw me in the pool?'

Adam shot a quick glance in the direction of the shimmering aqua depths. Then he turned to her with a lopsided smile that would have done strange things to her stomach if her pumping adrenalin had not already done the trick.

And this time, though he didn't say a word, he didn't need to.

'Don't you dare,' Cara whispered.

'Then don't tempt me, Cara.' His low, rumbling voice and his strong body spoke of all sorts of temptations that should have sent Cara running to her room.

'Give me the book and we both win,' he said.

Her pulse raced and she couldn't back down. 'No.'

His smile broadened. 'No?'

Letting temptation take rein, Cara again said, 'No.'

'Fine.'

His gaze raked over her body, which was trembling from an adrenalin overdose. She pictured her messy curls, her arms clamped over her chest, the sheer white shirt that stopped at her hips, leaving her black bikini bottom and bare legs available to his raking glance. She had no idea what was going through his mind, but no matter what it was she was struck still as a statue. But then when his hot gaze landed upon her knee it stopped. Cara followed the direction of his eyes and saw the scrape he had tended to the day before. It looked pretty raw. As did the massive bruise on her thigh that had come up overnight.

His gaze shot back to her face and she was shocked to see the raw alarm etched there. All evidence of playtime gone, he took a step around the sun lounger but she flinched, clasping the book to herself even tighter.

He slowed, but kept on coming. 'Cara, don't be ridiculous. I'm not throwing you in the pool now. Just let me look at you.'

Cara stood stock-still as he rounded the chair and came to her side, his hands held in front of him as though to calm a startled deer.

'That bruise is just insane. Have you seen a doctor?'

She shook her head.

He reached out as though to touch it and Cara jumped back, the thought of those warm fingers running down her thigh sending her adrenal glands into overdrive.

'Don't tell me Jeff won't let you see a doctor,' he growled. 'If they won't bring in someone from the outside I'll sure have something to say about it.' His gaze whipped from her to flick to the hotel-suite windows high above them.

Sensing that he was about to scale the building to get to Jeff, Cara reached out and took him by the arm to garner his attention. His gaze swung her way. She could not fathom its intensity.

'Adam, please. I'm fine. It's a bruise. That's what happens when a human throws themselves at an expanse of hardened dirt. The human invariably comes off second-best. And it looks worse than it feels, I promise. If I bump into something, which I do often, I bruise. This, though larger than normal, is nothing unusual.'

Adam swallowed as his gaze once more sought out the black and yellow expanse. How Cara wished she were fully dressed. Having anyone stare so closely at one's bare thighs was never a pleasant occurrence, and having Adam in all his perfect athletic glory do so felt more uncomfortable than usual. His gaze was so focussed she could feel it scorching her bare skin. It was too much.

Her hand moved from his lovely bicep to take him by the chin so she could physically stop him from staring at her legs. 'Adam. I'm fine. OK?'

After several moments of intense concentration he nodded and she could feel the light stubble on his chin move against her fingertips. Suddenly aching to run her fingers over his cheeks and mouth to learn their texture, she pulled her hand away. Adam grabbed at it before she could get away, his long fingers easily encircling her skinny wrist.

He then used his grip as leverage, pulling her closer to him. Caught as she was in his dilated gaze, she could do little but acquiesce.

'Adam…' she started.

'Shh.'

She shushed.

He brought her hand around behind him so that it was locked against his back and her hips were flush against his. She could feel the smooth hardness of his waist along her forearm. Her breathing slowed to match his, until it was leisurely and lingering.

Then just as Cara all but gave into the idea that this big, gorgeous man was actually going to kiss her, the big gorgeous man's other hand reached up and grabbed the book from her slackened grasp.

Letting go, he sprung to the other side of the sun lounger, and out of her reach. He scooped up his towel and flung it over his shoulder.

'Count yourself lucky, Cara,' he said, his dark eyes flashing all the warning she needed. 'I might not be so noble next time.'

Mouth tingling with thwarted expectations, Cara watched him go, having no idea if he meant that next time their lips might meet as she had so much wanted them to do, or that she would end up in the pool.

Either way she thought she'd got away pretty lightly.

CHAPTER SEVEN

MONDAY, during the Luna Park date, Cara was again able to work herself ragged, but only because Adam had thankfully made himself scarce. Chris mentioned something about phone calls and workloads and Cara thanked her lucky stars that she was afforded the time to concentrate on her job.

But the day was all she was given. That night, as Adam once more accompanied her and Chris in their limo, it took a concerted effort to act as though everything were hunky-dory, even though her pulse beat more rapidly every time she glanced his way.

'How are you holding up, buddy?' she asked Chris.

'Pretty well.'

'Good.' She patted his knee. 'You are doing just fine. Do you know what they have in store for you tonight?'

'Karaoke,' he said, his face pale.

'I take it you're no virtuoso?'

'I don't even sing in the shower.'

'Think of it as an adventure.'

At the word adventure she saw Chris turn an even more sickly shade of green.

'The roller coaster at Luna Park was bad enough. Stick a microphone in front of me and I will be physically ill. I can't even do any public speaking, can I, Adam? That's why I roped Adam into Revolution Wireless in the first place—he can do anything in public without breaking a sweat.'

The word 'anything' conjured up all sorts of bad, bad

images that Cara had to squash deep down inside her impertinent imagination.

Concentrating hard on Chris, she took hold of his hands. 'Chris, most people live their lives within walls. Within confines. Within boundaries. But you have been given an opportunity to branch out, to try new things, test yourself. This is a privilege and if I were you I would go out there and sing like you've never sung before. Don't look back on this time with any regrets. OK?'

The car remained silent and Cara wondered if she had pushed too far. Then Chris nodded as though he were letting the idea wash over him, letting it seep inside his suit until it became a part of his armour plating.

By the time the limo pulled up to the bar, Chris was out the door, eager as a schoolboy to get onto the playground.

'Nice speech you made in there,' Adam said as he helped Cara out of the car.

She drew her hand from his as soon as was polite. 'Thanks.'

'What would you do in his situation?'

She shot him a sideways glance. 'Hide in the ladies' room all night. Without a doubt.'

Adam laughed. It was deep and resonant and infectious. 'Not such a bad plan. But it was still a nice speech. Chris will have a much better night because of it.'

Cara shrugged. 'It's my job. It's up to me to have the character be the person the producers need him to be. And Chris will be a much better hero for our show if he goes out there and has fun.'

'So that's why you gave him the pep talk? All for the good of the show?'

'Mmm hmm.'

'Sure it was.' Adam slipped an arm about her torso and

gave her one quick squeeze. 'You are all class, Ms Marlowe.'

When he let go and went into the club, Cara stood stock-still and stared at his departing back. It was ridiculous. Her whole body was shaking. One small, chummy hug and he had her nerve endings rioting for more. And the funny thing was, it didn't feel like flirting any more.

He had called her classy. And she knew instinctively it was not in the same joking manner her friends used the word. It was a real compliment and he was not a guy who gave compliments easily. It felt like a mark of...friendship. She felt as if she were skimming across the water in a speedboat, shooting through the levels of a relationship, all too fast. While on the job. With a guy who did not know the meaning of the word relationship.

Cara knew that Adam, son and heir to a history of failed relationships, had no such intentions. If he saw her as anything it was as a quick bedding before breakfast. And she had the funny feeling that, though it would be a pretty darned nice experience on its own, she would not come out of it with the same nonchalance. He did things to her senses that gave her fair warning not to take it any further than it had already gone. As such, for the sake of her job, for the sake of her plans, for the sake of her inexperienced heart, it would be up to her to nip it in the bud before it went any further.

When Cara made it inside the club, the show was up and running already. Cara looked around and found Adam. She gravitated to him, as she always did. There was one other seat at his table and it had already been pulled out. For her.

Then and there she decided to do her bud-nipping later. After allowing herself to enjoy his complicated company under the cover of forgiving darkness for a little while longer.

She sat, and gave Adam a small smile. He smiled back. And in the darkness of the club, she felt her inexperienced heart flip over on itself.

A couple of hours later the party was in full swing. Chris and the girls had enjoyed a sumptuous Japanese dinner, including enough sake to lubricate their vocal cords. And then the karaoke machine lit up, a spotlight showcasing the microphone that stood alone and lonely mid-stage.

'Here we go,' Cara said under her breath and Adam saw her hands clenching and unclenching upon the table.

He reached out and placed a hand over hers, their fingers meshing together, hoping to settle her. But she only stiffened all the more. She was desperately nervous for Chris; he could feel it. Sincerely worried for him. Sincerely. That was not a word Adam had had cause to use before when referring to a woman in his life. He gently massaged her palm until he could tell she was relaxing.

He had reason enough to keep her happy, to keep her comfortable, to sit with her, to tell her when he thought she had done a good thing. He had to be nice to her for Chris's sake. For Chris and for the sake of the company.

But even as he thought it he realised how ridiculous it sounded.

There was no way he was gravitating to the woman every time she was in the room for *the good of the company*. He was gravitating towards her because he was caught in her gravitational force. He was like a moon spinning around her planet. The day spent making phone calls and shouldering a workload he could just as easily have shuffled onto someone else proved that.

Where she was, there he wanted to be. Not because he wanted to keep her in check, or because she was the life of the party. Not just because he felt an uncontrollable need to touch her whenever he had the chance, but because he also felt a deep-seated need to protect her. And that was the worst reason he could possibly have.

Disentangling his fingers, he stood, his chair scraping against the polished wood floor, earning several severe glances from the television crew.

'Where are you going?' Cara whispered, her husky voice washing over him in the darkness, and he felt something tugging deep within him at her concern.

There was only so much sincerity he could take before it began to make a subversive impact, so he didn't answer her, merely walked away, not caring about the shaft of light he let into the set as he stormed from the room and outside.

He took off up the street, feeling the need for fresh air. He needed something other than the heady, disturbing scent of flowers that seemed to have filled his nostrils and addled his brain ever since she had joined them in the car.

It was intoxicating. He was intoxicated. There could be no other explanation for the sensations creeping through his body and mind. No explanation. No excuse. No reason to let them get any further. He was not the type to fall prey to such intoxication. He'd had his last drink of that delicious scent and he had to give it up before he became addicted.

'You are being absurd,' he said out loud. 'Control yourself, man. You'll be out of this Petri dish in a week and a half, and then back out into the big wide world where a dozen other perfumes, much more sophisticated than hers will grab you in just the same way. And you'll want to grab them right back.'

Back in the karaoke bar, Cara stayed put. The suddenness of Adam's departure played on her and kept her from paying full attention to the show, but, though she had wanted to leap from her chair and follow Adam, she knew Chris needed her.

After several songs had been sung, Chris turned to Maggie and begged her to give it a go. Maggie had been sitting back quietly, her face as pale as Chris's had been in the car, while the other women had sung and danced and writhed about the stage for Chris's benefit.

'Come on, Maggie,' Chris insisted. 'I know most of these girls can sing like angels, but I'm no Pavarotti. Give it a go. You'll feel like a million bucks afterwards.'

Cara watched as Chris smiled at Maggie, his face aglow with confidence and something else again, a need to shield the girl, to make her feel safe, to overcome his own embarrassment to protect her from hers.

He took her by the hand and led her to the mike. 'You pick the song,' he offered, 'anything you like.'

She nodded, her long blonde hair falling over her shoulders, her bright blue eyes so wide, but trusting, since she had her hand in his.

And Cara knew that, no matter the great speech she had given, Chris had never been more in control than now. Now that he had to be brave for someone more fearful of public humiliation than he was. And though Cara knew Maggie was no country hick as she joked, she looked as if she had never held a microphone in her life.

Chris picked it up for her, put it into her hands and then moved to sit with the other girls.

The first strains of her song began, and Maggie looked wildly out into the crowd beyond the bright lights. Cara stood and moved beside the main camera in the middle of the set. Maggie's gaze flicked straight to her and there was a glimmer of recognition. Cara grinned widely and gave the girl two thumbs up.

Maggie brightened immeasurably, then said into the mike, 'Practice makes perfect, right?'

Cara looked over to Chris, who was grinning at Maggie proudly, and though all the other girls were doing their dandiest to grab his attention, he only had eyes for the one on stage.

'So here goes,' Maggie said, 'the musical stylings of Maggie O'Laughlan. Seen for the first time outside of third-grade choir. Hold onto your seats.'

Then, with a big wink at Chris that had him leaning forward and watching her as though she were the greatest thing ever to hold a mike, she serenaded him with the most off-key yet passionate rendition of 'Stand By Your Man' that anyone had ever heard. And it brought the house down. The cast, the crew, even the waiters gave her a standing ovation. And in the end Maggie fell, exhausted, mortified and exhilarated, into Chris's waiting arms.

Cara turned to look into the smiling faces of the crew and found Adam had returned. He was lurking in the dark doorway, leaning on the wall, his arms and ankles crossed and he was the only one in the place not smiling.

She wondered what on earth could have him looking so sullen. But since he was so decidedly staring her way, and not at the tableau before her, she knew without a doubt it had something to do with her.

Her stomach tightened in response. It wasn't nerves. It wasn't hunger. It was awareness. Pure, unadulterated, sexual awareness.

He was watching her as a tiger watched its prey and she was petrified that, if the time came, she wouldn't run for her life. She would bare her neck, ready for the kind of torture she just knew his attentions would impart. Sweet, delicious, mind-numbing torture.

When the next song started, Cara broke free of Adam's

eye contact and turned to face the singers. And there she stayed for the remainder of the shoot, her feet planted, her legs shaking, her whole body stiff with the pressure of holding her ground and not turning to seek out the one person she knew she should not want to seek out.

Especially under the veil of forgiving darkness that she had found so secretly comforting not long before.

Tuesday morning, Cara stood atop the grassy lawn of the Flemington Racecourse, level with the starting line, a betting slip clutched in her hot palm, her spare hand shielding her eyes from the bright sunshine.

'Come on, number eight!' Cara cried out, her silver bangles clinking as she bounced up and down on her tiptoes to see over the dozens of heads in between her and the magnificent racehorses rounding the straight.

She had almost left her strappy white shoes behind on a number of occasions, the spiky heels all but disappearing into the moist turf with each step. And though the hat she had hastily created the night before—a simple conglomeration of mesh, white satin, a few feathers and netting, cocked jauntily to the side—matched her black and white lace dress perfectly, it created no shade whatsoever and she knew her nose would be spattered with freckles by the end of the day.

'Go, you good thing. Bring Papa home the bacon!' Jeff added, leaping up and down at her side.

Cara watched as both their hopes and dreams faded when number eight came home somewhere in the middle of the pack.

'Oh, well,' Jeff said, his frown turning upside down quick smart, 'at least he didn't come last. We are improving.'

'That we are,' Cara agreed. 'The odds are obviously on our side. By the time the Melbourne Cup comes around we're sure to come home with a win.'

Jeff nodded, satisfied. Then his finger moved to his right ear and Cara knew a message was being beamed down to him through his hidden earpiece. 'The girls are here. Is Chris ready?'

'Just about. I'll go make sure.' Cara headed to the back of their private marquee to find Chris, who was secreted away in his own little air-conditioned mini tent.

'Howdy, Chris.'

Chris turned, his face relaxing instantly at the sight of her. She leaned in, gave him a big kiss on the cheek, then continued to run both hands down his jacketed arms.

'How you feeling, buddy?'

'Fine.'

'Only fine? Because you are looking absolutely divine. Those ladies are going to go gaga when you walk out there looking so damn fine.'

She shuffled in behind him, her arms around his neck fixing his tie with adept hands, so they were both looking in the full-length mirror. She gave him a wink and a solid grin and felt her job was done when he smiled back.

It was only when her gaze moved from his reflection to her own that she saw they were not alone. She spun to face the man sitting quietly on a chair in the corner.

'Adam,' she said, her voice breathier than she would have liked. 'I didn't see you there.'

'That's the way he likes it, I'm afraid,' Chris scoffed. 'He would rather be the silent witness, looking down upon us all, than be in the game himself. Isn't that right, Adam?'

'Who am I to disagree?' he said, his face its usual hidden self.

'That surprises me,' Cara said, talking to Chris but with her gaze firmly fixed on the man sitting so casually in the chair. Maybe this was the perfect opportunity to call him out. To set some ground rules using Chris as an unknowing chaperon. 'From what I have heard and read, I would have thought Adam was a player.'

'Oh, he does well enough with the ladies. But they never seem to stick around too long.'

'Hmm. And why would that be, do you think?'

Cara could feel the heat emanating from Adam, even at her safe distance. His energy levels were growing exponentially as they talked about him. She just knew that he was dying to tell them both to lay off, but that would mean breaking down his permanent air of indifference.

'Well,' Chris said, 'that would be because our young friend has no intention of letting them stick around too long. The last of the confirmed bachelors, is our Adam.'

She remembered the passage she had read about in the 'Unauthorised' book. A guy from a broken home. A guy whose father had flaunted his lovers all his life. She had heard the reasons for his indifference to settling down too many times from enough sources not to believe it.

But the fire pulsing from those blue eyes became too much for Cara. She had the distinct feeling if she pushed much further she might get burnt. She turned away, bringing her attentions back to an easier target.

'Unlike you, hey, Chris?'

'Absolutely. I'm lookin' for love in all the right places.'

'That's my boy.'

'So, how about you, Cara?' Chris asked. 'Is there a man on the outside, avidly awaiting your return?'

Cara sensed a shift in Adam's posture. She flicked a glance his way and found he had uncrossed his legs and was leaning forward with his elbows resting on his knees. He wanted to know the answer and he was showcasing the fact. And now was the time to let him know it was never going to be any of his business.

'No, there's not, Chris. But I guess you could call me the last of the confirmed bachelorettes.'

'Really? That seems a dreadful pity. A girl like you could make some man very happy. Don't you agree, Adam?'

'Or not, as the case may be,' Cara bit off before Adam had the chance to even think about framing an answer. 'So long as I am not making someone out there unhappy, then that's enough for me. Besides, I am a woman with very specific plans for my future, and the last thing I need is something or someone coming along and messing up those plans.'

'What plans could a romantic interest mess up, do you think, Adam?' Chris said, his expression playful.

'Maybe she wants to be Miss Australia,' Adam said.

Cara shot him her most disparaging glare. 'You got me in one. I wanna be a beauty queen.'

'You'd get my vote.'

That shut Cara up quick smart. She turned back towards safer waters. 'OK, Chris. Enough mucking about. It's time to roll.'

She smoothed down the shoulders of Chris's jacket, flicked practised fingers through his hair and straightened the flower in his buttonhole. With a soft click of her cheek, she gave Chris a big smile.

'Looks like I'll be on clean-up duty for the rest of the day. I'll be following after those women out there wiping up their drool.'

Chris grimaced.

Jeff poked his head in the tent. 'OK, sports fans. Let's do it.'

Cara spun Chris on the spot and with two hands in the middle of his back gave him a nice shove towards the door flap. Once outside in the light of day, Chris was no longer hers as he disappeared into the swarming crew.

Cara felt Adam sidle up beside her.

'Looks like it's just you and me again,' he said.

Cara shrugged, more to give herself the chance to shake off the same old strain that always came upon her when he was so close.

Obviously telling him and herself the attraction resonating between them would come to no good simply wasn't working. It was like throwing a thimbleful of water on a bushfire. So then and there she made a decision to befriend the enemy, hoping it would make him less unnerving. Less intriguing. Less affecting. She would treat him as a mate, in the hopes it would make him as likely to sweep her off her feet as Jeff. Perish the thought!

'Looks that way,' she said, looping an arm through his. 'So I guess we'll have to bear it with what grace we can. Come on, you can buy me a drink.'

'It's an open bar,' he said, his feet planted, his tone even more stoic than usual.

She had no choice but to look him in the eye. 'The sun is shining. It's the Melbourne Cup. We are in a private tent, being waited on by men with weird food and goldfish bowls on their trays, so I am looking to take advantage and have an all-round fabulous day. Are you going to work with me here or not?'

His cool expression finally melted and Cara was rewarded with a hint of one of those rare, thus all the more enjoyed for the having, smiles.

And the reaction it caused in her stomach was almost enough for her to wish she could take back her little rant and keep to the other side of the tent alone all day. Almost.

'OK, boss,' he said, tucking her hand more securely through his arm. 'An all-round fabulous day coming up.'

*   *   *

When the big race came, the crowd moved forward as one. The Melbourne Cup had begun. Every person in Australia stopped what they were doing, turned to their televisions or their radios or the racecourse in front of them. Every person in the country stopped, watched and screamed their lungs out.

Every person except Adam, whose eyes remained steadfastly locked onto the back of the woman in the black and white dress, leaping about amidst the crowd of cast and crew before him.

She had been talking to him earlier, when she was chatting to Chris about not looking for romance, he had been sure of it. He had her running scared, before anything more had even happened between them than some light teasing and a few stray chances at touching one another. Cara was very determinedly trying to keep their relationship professional, even though she still flinched as if she had been burned every time they brushed within an inch of one another. And that sort of awareness should not be ignored. It had promise.

So what was the big problem?

The problem was Adam felt an attraction to her so strong he could all but see the ropes binding them together, but he also felt frustratingly disconnected. She was tough with Jeff, encouraging with the girls, a mate to the crew and a rock for Chris. But with him she was like vapour. Ephemeral, changeable, out of reach. And he knew there was no way he could stand another week watching her give everyone else exactly what they needed, except him.

The horses rounded the straight and the crescendo of noise and heat swelled around him. But Adam couldn't have cared less. He wanted nothing more than to drag Cara back into the private room at the rear. To have her all to himself. He willed her to turn, to look back at him, to smile, to understand. But she did not. She bounced up and down, her eyes firmly fixed on the race before her.

'Yippee!' a familiar husky voice called out, dragging Adam from his reverie. 'It only took all bloody day but I finally picked a winner! I've never won anything. Ever! Not even a school fête raffle!'

Weaving her way through the dispersing crowd, Cara tumbled over to him and threw herself so wholly into his arms her feet no longer touched the ground. Adam baulked. He finally had what he wanted. She was in his arms, but he didn't know what to do with her.

She felt so fragile and soft. So energetic and young. And he was completely overwhelmed.

'So how much did you win, Cara?' Adam asked when she finally stopped bouncing.

Cara stood on tiptoe, shielding her eyes from the sun as the final odds came up on the big screen. 'I won…twelve dollars and fifteen cents.'

After a brief pause Adam asked, 'That's it?'

'I only put down a fifty-cent bet.'

'And that's enough to get you into such a state?'

'I'm a girl who's learnt to take her joy wherever she can get it.'

Adam looked down into her smiling face and he knew she was also a girl who knew what she was talking about.

Her arms were slung casually around his neck, one hand buried deep in his hair, the other tucking under the collar of his shirt. Above the scent of her freshly applied sunscreen Adam noticed the mixed scents of cut grass and her usual floral perfume wafting on the warm air. And everything suddenly became clear.

If he was looking for a moment of joy to remember, to

cling to, to revisit, this was it. He took the time to burn the imprint of the moment onto his memory.

The desire to kiss her swept over him, and, for a guy who lived by the control he had over his faculties, the feeling was overpowering. No matter that it would have her running to the hills before he even had the chance to finesse her; her smiling face, her pliant, warm body, the sweet scent of champagne on her breath, the whole kit and caboodle inundated him to the extent that his head began to spin. His head that was of its own accord lowering to hers.

Then, before he could finally taste of those sweet lips, she was wrenched from his arms by a very insistent Jeff.

'Come on, my little winner, I need to rub you for good luck. Tell me who's going to win on the next race.'

Cara shot a forgive-me grin over her shoulder as she was bundled off towards their bookie.

It was the second time they had almost kissed, and the hundredth time he had wanted to do it. What on earth was happening to him? If he saw someone he wanted this much, he went for it. Always. So what was the problem? He knew with every faltering breath and every flicker of those expressive green eyes that she was just as attracted to him, no matter how much she was trying to tell herself she wasn't. So what? What was stopping him from simply taking what he wanted, consequences be damned?

She was nothing like the sort of woman his father kept; she preferred a flower in her hair to jewels around her neck and he would have put money on the fact that her caramel-coloured hair was as close to its natural colour as that of any woman he had met, and that those curls were all hers.

Still, she could be a wolf in sheep's clothing. But if that were true, would that fact make her less datable or more so? Adam could barely remember any more, he had put such strict and overlapping boundaries on himself when it came to his relationships with women.

With every step that his business grew, he added a brick to the wall around his heart. And this one, without even trying, made him care so little about the consequences of his actions he wanted to take a sledgehammer to the whole thing so he could just start afresh.

Adam shoved his hands deep within his trouser pockets and stormed off to find himself the greatest gulp of fresh air he had ever needed.

CHAPTER EIGHT

AT THE end of the day, all of the key crew ended up in Chris's suite back at the Ivy Hotel with Cara hanging onto Chris at the front of the conga line.

'Three cheers for the winner!' Chris shouted.

Cara gave the cheering mob a tipsy pirouette. 'Thank you. Thank you all. And I want to let you know that I plan on using my twelve dollars and fifteen cents only for the greater good. Money will not change me. I will still look down on you as ants to be crushed beneath my feet as I always have.' She gave them a nice deep curtsy, before collapsing onto the couch, her wide, multi-layered skirt puffing out around her.

Adam followed behind, ever the big brother, the watcher, standing on the outside looking in. He shut the door behind them, as the gang obviously had no thought for such sensibilities.

'Yet twelve dollars and fifteen cents does not a fortune make,' Cara said thoughtfully.

Adam pulled out one of the dining chairs and turned it to face the sunken lounge. He sat down, leant an elbow on the dining table, and rested his head against his hand. And he watched the interplay before him.

'True,' Chris said, smiling companionably at Cara. 'It will hardly pay off one's university loan.'

Cara fluffed a hand at Chris. 'All paid off.'

Adam paid closer attention.

'Really?' Chris asked, his voice also a little giddy from

champagne, sunshine and something else Adam could not put his finger on. 'OK, then, what about your car loan?'

'Paid off.'

'My, my. Home loan, then?'

Cara opened her mouth, then closed it. 'Not quite,' she finally said, grinning sheepishly. She then held up her hand, squinting through a tiny sliver of light that could be seen between her forefinger and thumb. 'But I am this close.'

She leaned over and in a loud stage whisper declared to the world, 'You know what else? My parents rented their entire lives. Never owned a house. Never owned a car. And in a little over a week, when I get my pay for this magnificent gig, I will have both. Not bad, eh?' She nodded, obviously mightily impressed with herself.

Chris nodded along with her. 'Not bad at all. And how old are you?'

'Not yet twenty-seven and not, may I add, a part owner in a multibillion-dollar company.'

Chris grinned back. 'Well, good for you. The styling business must be more lucrative than I thought.'

'Perhaps a very little,' she said with a self-deprecating giggle. 'I learnt early that, though twelve dollars will not quite get me my building, every cent helps.'

Chris nodded sagely, his head wobbling slightly on his neck. 'Makes sense to me.'

Adam ran a hand through his hair. The talk of money had him shifting in his seat. Her face took on a whole new look when she spoke of cents and dollars. It glowed with determination. He had seen something akin to that look many times over and it always made him uncomfortable.

But this was different. This one was determined to do it on her own. And that was what was making him itch. If she really came from nothing as she professed, then why the hell wasn't she throwing herself on his mercy? How much could she possibly be earning from the gig? A few thousand at most. A pittance to Adam. She had him so stirred up, if she played her cards right she could get pretty much whatever she wanted from him. At that nauseating realisation, Adam's itch got worse.

'Besides which, I wouldn't say I was the big winner of the day.' Cara pulled herself from her chair and shuffled over to Chris, plopping herself on his lap.

Adam sat up straighter at this sudden move. If he thought the talk of money made him uncomfortable, seeing Cara sitting on his best friend's lap made his jaw clench so tight he half expected to taste blood.

He wrenched himself from his chair and began to pace the room.

'I would say that young Christopher here was our big winner,' Cara continued, pinching Chris on both cheeks.

Jeff and the other crew, who had been more intrigued by the contents of Chris's mini-bar than by the conversation at hand, suddenly joined in.

'Hear, hear,' Jeff agreed, holding up a glass of something brown and alcoholic.

'What?' Chris said, his neck turning red.

'It is so obvious,' Cara gushed. 'You are a goner. You are in lurve.'

'Am I even allowed to talk about this?' Chris asked, looking to Jeff for help.

Jeff shrugged. 'So long as it's only between us, I don't see why not. Go for your life.'

'I know who Chris likes,' Cara chanted. 'I know who Chris likes.'

Adam stopped his pacing. He turned and watched. Waiting. Suddenly it didn't matter to him that Chris was falling from his protective reach. It just mattered to him that the conversation be finished as soon as possible so that Cara would disembark from his friend's lap.

Cara leaned down and whispered in Chris's ear and Chris blushed madly. He looked back at her, his face changed, filled with wonder and delight. And Adam stood stock-still with shock. Chris was not just falling. He had fallen. Chris was in love.

Adam's head began to spin. It was fast becoming too much to take on. But what could he do? Nothing. Just stand there and take it all in. Standing on the outside looking in had suddenly taken on a whole new meaning. He was simply out of the loop.

Adam cringed as a great rocking INXS song suddenly blared out of the hidden speakers. Jeff had found the stereo. The whole gang joined in, singing happily at the tops of their lungs. Cara leapt from Chris's lap and dragged him from the chair. They danced about the room, with each other, alone, as a group, copying each other's muddled steps. Cara, as the only woman in the room, had the most attention as the guys took it in turn to twirl her in their arms.

And though she was not the most coordinated person on a sporting field, and though Adam was more than sure that she walked extra carefully when wearing heels more than an inch high, she was one heck of a dancer. The music did something to her, gave her confidence, or perhaps some kind of shield so that she could just let go. Her lithe body spoke of the poise of a ballet dancer and it did not disappoint. She was graceful, and the pulsing tempo of the song sang through her limbs.

Then the music changed. A slow number ensued. The gents partnered up, stumbling, twirling each other about the room. Cara and Jeff joined in, both leading and both following in a ridiculous mimicking imitation of a ballroom-dancing exhibition.

That was as much as Adam could take. He stormed down to the makeshift dance floor and tapped Jeff on the shoulder. Jeff turned to him, and it took a few moments for understanding to dawn. Then he departed with a gallant bow leaving Cara standing, puffing slightly, her green eyes bright and dancing themselves. Adam reached out and took Cara into his arms. And without a word she came to him.

She rested her heavy head on his shoulder and swayed jauntily to the beat. Adam slowed her down, leading until she followed, her feet stopped jitterbugging and eventually she just swayed. She hummed, the sound vibrating through his chest, her sweet voice lilting and tripping across the chords of the song.

It was all he could do to stop himself from holding her tighter still. To wish that the room would clear. To have the sun set and leave them in the darkened space, alone.

'What did you say to Chris earlier?' he asked, his voice low and solemn.

Cara lifted her head from his shoulder. 'Hmm?' She looked at him with a blissful smile on her face.

And what a face. Pretty, pale, a smattering of freckles darkened lightly by their day in the sun, small upturned nose, long eyelashes framing her gorgeous green eyes, and lips that were made for kissing.

It took Adam more than a moment to recall his thoughts.

'Chris,' he remembered. 'I was wondering what you said to Chris that had him look so happy.'

'Oh. That.' She leaned in closer so as to whisper to him. Adam could smell the sweet scent of strawberries and champagne on her lips. It was about as much as he could bear. 'I told him I thought she was just lovely.'

'Who?' he croaked.

'The woman who makes him smile.'

'And who is that?'

She pulled back and waggled a finger at him. 'I can't say. It wouldn't be fair. Though I am a hundred per cent sure that I know who she is, it is not up to me to lead him her way. It is up to him to decide who the woman is who would make him most happy.'

'So how can you be sure you know who it is?'

She raised one eyebrow, one side of her lips kicking up in a wry smile creating the gorgeous smile line in her right cheek. 'Are you serious? Are you really telling me that you haven't seen the signs?'

'What signs?'

'The signs! The fact that he has slowed down immeasurably. He's not so nervous any more. He smiles for no reason. He looks at least half a foot taller. He doesn't whinge when we shave his chest any more. The signs!'

Adam had seen them all right, but he had been so distracted by...other things that they had passed him by.

'OK. So I've seen the signs. Which one is she? The chesty redhead? The blonde who laughs like a donkey? Don't tell me it's the cross-eyed brunette.'

Cara slapped him on the chest then her hand remained resting there, just above his heart, and it was almost enough to distract him anew. He swallowed hard.

'So what if it was one of those girls?' Cara asked. 'If they make him smile, make him relax, make him happy, does it really matter?'

'So long as they treat him well,' Adam said, and was shocked to hear the words spill from his own mouth.

'Exactly. And I know that this girl feels the same for him.'

'How?'

She rolled her eyes, then her hand slipped up from his

chest to take him by the chin, drawing his focus back to her face and nothing else. 'The signs, silly. The signs.'

The music stopped.

The sun had set.

The room had cleared.

They were alone.

Somehow in the last few minutes, while his attention had been so caught up in her alone, the crew had crept quietly from the room. Even Chris was nowhere to be seen and it was his room. Their swaying stopped.

'Where is everybody?' Cara's hand fell away, leaving his jaw cool where her fingers had made it warm.

'Gone,' he said.

'But why?'

Maybe they thought we might like some privacy! he ached to scream at her, knowing that would hardly help the situation.

'I couldn't rightly say.' He let her go and she leapt to a point far enough away that he could no longer feel her warmth. Her hands were wringing and she obviously didn't know where to rest her gaze.

'Would you like a drink?' he asked, already knowing the answer. She shook her head.

'I think I'd better go. I think I stayed long enough.' Her hand moved to cover her stomach. 'I think I drank and ate too much and had too much sun. And I think I had better lie down.'

Her face was beginning to look a little green.

'It's OK, Cara. Go lie down. I'll get Room Service to send you up some Berocca and dry toast.'

'Are you sure?' she asked. 'I'm sorry to have ruined your party.'

Adam looked around at the mess the crew had left in their wake. Finding the beseeching look in those green eyes too much to bear, he spun her on the spot and pushed her from the room. 'Goodnight, Cara. Sweet dreams.'

And the look she sent him as he closed the door showed him exactly what those dreams would be. The green around her dilated pupils blazed, and it was only her hand resting lightly on her aching stomach that stopped him from wrenching her back into the room and making those very dreams come true.

Cara spent the next few days as far from Adam's company as she could. It was bad enough hearing that the crew had a pool going to see who could correctly guess what had happened once they'd left Chris's room, but having to face him with the remembrance of swaying in his arms imprinted all along her body was even worse. But thankfully he seemed to have found a lot of work to do regarding the show's sponsorship, thus had turned up on set but rarely.

He had to know that he had her affections in the palm of his hand. She couldn't even perk up the courage to try to be mates again. She had blown that ruse all too quickly by melting into his arms the minute she'd had the chance. Distance was best. Distance would make her feelings ease away, eventually. It simply had to.

So, by Saturday night, Cara was overjoyed when her best girls turned up to her hotel room for Saturday Night Cocktails.

'Wow,' Gracie said as she trundled into the hotel room, her eyes bright. 'I can't believe the security in this place. I was all prepared for a strip search and everything. If we didn't have these little pass thingies you sent us, I fear we might have been shot.'

'You're not kidding,' Cara said, knowing she had at least one tale she could share with her friends without breaking any contractual secrecy. Her cotton underwear story would

make the 'best-of' list, she feared. Especially since Gracie
and her jingling card were mainly to blame.

Gracie then turned to the doorway and beat a drum roll
on her thighs. 'And if that's not news enough for you,
Kelly's back from her trip with Simon to Fremantle.
Heeeeere's Kell-Belle!'

Kelly came through the door with a, 'Ta da!'

She gave Cara a much-needed hug and Cara hugged her
back. 'You look great!'

Kelly smiled. 'And how the heck are you?'

'You first,' Cara said, carefully deflecting the attention
away from herself. She hadn't yet figured what she was
going to tell her friends about…her last few days. 'How
was Fremantle, Kell?'

'Good. Simon had to head over there to do some business
so I decided to tag along. We caught up with his best man
and I had the chance to meet some of the friends he made
when he lived there. We had perfect weather. We stayed
in an amazing resort. It was simply wonderful.'

Gracie raised her dark eyebrows. 'Ahh the loving wife!
All's well between you two then?'

'*Really* good.' Kelly said with a charmed sigh that soon
dissolved within an accompanying blush.

Gracie squealed. 'Oh no, don't get too gooey on us now,
Kell-Belle. Soon all you'll have to offer the Saturday Night
Cocktails gang will be crochet patterns. Cara, I'm counting
on you to keep us in the real world. Do you have anything
to report? Or is the cone of silence still in place?'

'It is, I'm afraid,' Cara said. 'Despite the pass thingies.
But I can tell you the experience has been…more than I
even hoped it would be.'

'I am so proud of you, Cara,' Kelly said as Gracie gave
up on the details and went to check out the mini-bar. 'Soon
you will barely remember our names. We'll wave to you

as you trawl the red carpets of the world and you'll look over, recognise us, almost, searching through your memory, clutching at the brief glimmer that you may have met us once.'

Cara finally stopped Kelly by placing a hand firmly over her mouth. 'Stop it! Seriously, though, it's really the same job with video cameras rather than still cameras.'

'And more money, I hope? Don't shoot down that fantasy, too!'

'And more money,' Cara agreed, her stomach warming at the thought of owning St Kilda Storeys entirely within the next few days. So far she had not managed to embarrass herself into losing her job, slow dance with the show's sponsor notwithstanding.

'High five to more money,' Gracie joined in, holding up a hand ready to be slapped. When she was rewarded as such she said, 'How are we going to do this? The mini-bar is stocked with enough to give us about half a cocktail each. Shall we order Room Service, or what?'

'I've seen enough of the inside of this hotel room to last me a lifetime,' Cara said, 'so I thought we would trawl the hotel bar. And I've checked with my bouncer friends and they said it's fine. No interlopers allowed so we can play there.'

'Good idea,' Kelly said.

'But do remember, I have vouched for you guys. Be good. Do me proud. And whatever you might accidentally learn while here is to remain top secret. This is really important to me so—'

'Yadda, yadda, yadda,' Kelly said. 'Lips shut tight. Besides I have something else to tell you that's a heck of a lot more interesting than some nameless television show. We have something to really celebrate tonight.'

The tone in Kelly's voice stopped Cara cold.

'And what's that?'

'Simon and I are going to have a baby.'

Out of the corner of her eye, Cara saw Gracie's mouth flop open and she knew she was doing just as good a fish impression herself. The two of them threw themselves at Kelly.

'Kell-Belle!' Gracie squealed. 'That's fantastic!'

'Kelly, that is the best news ever,' Cara yelled into Kelly's ear.

When she finally extricated herself from the octopus arms of her friends, Kelly said, 'All I can say is thank goodness for these pass thingies. If they hadn't let me in tonight I would have scaled the walls to find you. And I'm not sure that Simon would have been impressed.'

'Neither would I,' Cara insisted. 'By order of the Saturday Night Cocktails gang there will be no wall-scaling in your immediate future.'

'And no cocktails,' Gracie piped in.

'But still lots of celebrations,' Kelly said. 'Come on, girls, let's hit the bar. And the first round of apple juice is on me!'

'So everything's cool?' Chris asked, leaning back in the dining chair in the hotel restaurant.

Dean nodded. 'All chugging away nicely. The news about this show must be locked up real tight, as nothing has leaked at all. Our share prices are still steady.'

Adam nodded, soaking in the business talk like a much-missed elixir. It was trackable. It made sense. 'We'll know the minute the news hits the streets. There'll be a bump to be sure.'

'You mean you don't think the shareholders will think I've gone mad and all jump ship?' Chris asked, his tongue firmly planted in his cheek.

Adam had the good grace to grin. 'My sponsorship deal will make us bucketloads, mate, despite the fact that you are as mad as a snake.'

Adam, Dean and Chris all looked up as a threesome of laughing young women spilled from the lift and made their way across the empty foyer to the hotel bar.

But Adam's gaze slammed to a halt once it hit Cara. She looked amazing in a chic white sleeveless top, a black knee-length skirt that clung to every curve and those seductive red shoes that did disquieting things to her walk. Her hair had been blow-dried straight and pulled back into a low pony-tail, a flirty fringe stopping just short of her lashes. She looked so unbelievably lovely Adam's peaceful mood disappeared in an instant and his body began to twitch with discomfort.

'Tell me they are some of your choices, buddy,' Dean begged in a soft, distracted voice, 'and I'll be on your side against Adam come hell or high water.'

Chris laughed. 'Sorry, Dean. The taller one in the middle is my stylist for the show, the other two I don't know. Shall I call them over?'

'No, leave them be—' Adam began but it was too late. They had been spotted. So much for a night of business talk to get his head straightened out.

'Cara!' Chris called out, standing and waving.

Cara glanced their way and smiled. Adam was hit with that same light-hearted sensation that still took him by surprise every time she came into view.

Adam stood as the ladies approached. And Cara's smile faltered the instant it landed on him.

'Won't you and your friends join us, please?' Chris asked.

'Three girls, three boys. This is just trouble waiting to happen,' said one of Cara's friends, a curvy brunette in a tight red dress. The other friend in the denim jacket slapped her on the arm but could not control her indulgent smile.

'Good evening, Chris,' Cara said, giving him a great hug. When she pulled away her gaze remained resolutely anywhere but upon Adam.

'And you must be Dean,' she said, reaching over to shake the other man's hand. Adam watched as his friend all but melted under her sweet smile.

Finally she had no choice but to turn his way.

'Adam,' she said, leaning over to place a feather-light kiss upon his cheek.

He closed his eyes. He couldn't help himself. He was better able to breathe deep of the moment, to memorise the supple softness of cheek against his, her light floral perfume, the brief grip of her small hand upon his arm.

When he opened his eyes she was pulling away and he was startled to find her eyes were closed too. She blinked them open as though she were becoming used to a suddenly bright light. Their green depths sparkled, crinkling at the edges for a moment as though questioning...what?

Then she bit her lip and pulled away, physically and mentally, all but hiding herself behind her friends as she made her introductions.

'The one with the mouth is Gracie Lane,' Cara said. 'She's a croupier in the high rollers room at Crown Casino.'

'My advice is always choose red,' Gracie of the curves and tight dress said, giving a little curtsy as she shook hands with each of the gents.

Adam watched in amazement as quiet, workaholic Dean all but split a seam to get to her first. 'It suits you,' he said, his ears turning the same colour as Gracie's dress.

'Hey,' Gracie suddenly said, pointing an accusing finger at Adam.

'Yes?'

'You're not Adam Tyler, are you?'

Adam nodded, then shook his head, not sure which bit of the question to answer first. Then, to avoid further confusion, he said, 'I am he.'

'Wow!' She grabbed Cara's other friend by the arm and tugged several times. 'This is the guy who replaced you and Simon as the most photographed couple in *Fresh* magazine's social pages after your wedding. Though of course he was the only constant in the couple, changing the girl on his arm as regularly as he changed his tie.'

Gracie looked back at Adam, with one eyebrow cocked cheekily as though daring him to deny it. He shrugged his response, which earned him a huge grin from Gracie, who looked around the room.

'No new girl tonight?'

He shook his head and this time kept his mouth shut.

Her smile grew. 'Fabulous! Then this should make for one heck of an evening.'

'If you're done, Gracie...' Cara said.

Gracie linked her spare arm through Cara's. 'For the moment.'

Adam noticed that Cara looked a little flushed. It seemed these friends of hers were even more outspoken than she was. And that certainly did bode for an interesting evening. 'And this is Kelly Coleman,' Cara said. 'Ever since she got back from honeymoon a few months ago, she's been writing an insanely popular column called *Married, and Loving It* in *Fresh* magazine.'

'Coleman is her married name. She's married,' Gracie reiterated swiftly, eyeing off each of the men individually. 'And pregnant.'

Cara and Kelly both shot Gracie a look that said, *Shut your mouth now.*

'Sorry. But at least now we can celebrate in style without having to tiptoe around the issue.'

'You couldn't tiptoe if your life depended on it, Gracie,' Kelly said.

Introductions complete, Adam said, 'Dean, why don't you fix us up with a larger table? And, Chris, order some drinks.'

'Cocktails,' Gracie insisted.

'Apple juice,' Cara interrupted quickly.

'Apple juice it is,' Dean promised with a grin.

Once the table was set, they took their places, with Cara calling the shots. Boy girl, boy girl, boy girl, she ordered.

She had somehow managed to take the seat farthest from Adam, and he had the feeling it had been entirely deliberate.

CHAPTER NINE

WHEN their drinks arrived, *sparkling* apple juice with little umbrellas, no less, and they had ordered a round of potato wedges with sour cream and guacamole, the small spontaneous party settled into a companionable rhythm.

'Well, since we can't talk about the reason why we are all here, what can we talk about?' Gracie asked.

Chris piped up. 'How about you tell us all about young Cara here? She's a quiet one. Keeps herself under wraps. She must know every last detail about my life but I know nothing at all about her.'

'What do you want to know?' Kelly asked, her eyes sparkling.

'No, please,' Cara begged. 'I am seriously uninteresting.'

Adam blinked as she shot a glance his way. Even though the gang as a whole was relaxed, she was on edge. And by that glance he knew it was because of him. It was strangely comforting to know he wasn't the only one who felt as if he were teetering on the edge of some inexplicable abyss.

'Does she have a middle name? Did she have braces as a child?' Chris asked. 'How old was she when she lost—?'

'Yes. No. And none of your business!' Cara shouted.

'I was going to say when she lost her first tooth!'

'Sure you were.'

Chris reached out and gave Cara a chummy one-armed hug and she blushed adorably under the attention. Adam shuffled in his chair, knowing there was no way he could ever do that with her now, just reach out and hug her like that. It was as though as soon as their skin touched they were both scorched by the contact. He was achingly envious of his friend and his easy way with her. Even though he knew she saw Chris as nothing more than a friend, it was still a much more evolved relationship than the two of them had.

'What about her love life?' Chris asked, with his arm still casually draped over her shoulder. 'She tells me there is no one out in the real world, but I can't believe that. She's just such a doll.'

Adam saw Cara shoot her friends a death stare that would have stopped him in his tracks but they poked their tongues out in the face of such rubbish.

'Believe it,' Kelly said. 'But if there was someone, he would be a puppy dog.'

'All slobber and mess on the carpet?' Dean asked.

The girls cracked up, though Cara buried her head in her hands, obviously knowing there was no point in trying to stop her friends once they were on a roll.

'Oh, no,' Kelly said. 'That would be more trouble than they were worth. I mean that she goes for guys who are sweet and accommodating. Guys who do as they are told.'

'Come on, that's not true,' Cara said.

'Please,' Gracie said, shifting straight to the edge of her seat. 'Name me one guy you've dated who has ever said no to you and lasted another day.'

Cara's mouth opened, then snapped shut tight.

Gracie grinned. 'Yet, even though we have a distinct pattern in young Cara's preferences, she has never settled down with a puppy dog yet.'

'Right you are,' Kelly said. 'Maybe there's something in that. Maybe what she really needs is an anti-puppy dog. Maybe what she really needs is someone with the strength to tell her to *stay*.'

Adam watched as Cara's hunted gaze flickered from Kelly to Gracie before settling on him with a force that slammed him against the back of his chair.

He knew he was no puppy dog, far from it. And she obviously thought the same thing. And though she verbally denied the gist of the entire conversation, in that one look he knew that she knew they were onto something.

Cara was a woman who until now had dated yes-men.

Adam was anything but.

Cara was a woman who would unquestionably blossom in the arms of someone whose strength and will matched her own.

And Adam was such a man.

So what did she expect him to do about it?

Cara couldn't handle another second sitting across from Adam. She had placed him there thinking it would be more comfortable than having to avoid brushing against his arm as they ate. But having him sitting directly across from her meant that she had no choice but to make constant eye contact. And those eyes of his spoke volumes she had no intention of indulging.

'Since you guys are obviously planning on talking a lot, how about another round of drinks to wet your whistles?' she asked, and as soon as she received one nod she was on her feet and hastening to the bar.

She leaned against the bar, her fingernails digging into the cool wood surface. The barman was nowhere to be seen but Cara didn't mind. She was enjoying the moment's peace.

'Hi,' Adam said as he ambled up next to her, and Cara all but jumped out of her skin.

'Hi,' she said back, her voice instantly husky.

'I like your friends.'

That was not what she had expected. She turned to him,

checking to see if he was playing her, but he was casually checking out the labels on the bottles above the bar.

'So do I. They mean the world to me.'

'The sisters you never had?'

Cara blinked. Then nodded. He was right. More than right. His arrow had landed dead centre. 'How did you know that?'

He shrugged. 'It seems to be how the world turns nowadays. The friends we make as adults become our new family. Especially for we confirmed singles.'

He shot her a wry smile and Cara could not help but smile back. But then something began to shift in his eyes, and she felt him pulling away. She had to stop herself from reaching out and grabbing him by the chin, beseeching him to stay with her.

'It's the great marketing key,' he continued, his voice heading back from soft and friendly to professional and aloof. 'Aim to hook the urban family or the hometown family. Pick your mark and play for it.'

'And you guys picked the new urban family?'

'We did.'

'Because you knew about it, right? Because you and Chris and Dean are in the same boat? Finding more in common, finding more solace, and more support from them than from your actual relatives?'

He shrugged and stiffened, the light finally extinguishing in his eyes. 'We chose that as our market share as nobody else had.'

Cara could not help but stiffen in response. Her whole body, which had relaxed at the first sign of an intimate conversation, surged back to high alert.

It was agony. The moments where he seemed to come out of his shell were enlightening. They drew her to him like nothing else she had ever experienced. He was intriguing, sensitive, and riveting. And she knew that she opened up to that side of him without even trying. Her whole body melted and relaxed.

And then when he pulled away, emotionally and mentally, she became like a cat on a hot tin roof, skittish and anxious and ready to flee.

Probably best that way. As Gracie had so blatantly pointed out earlier, this guy was a playboy. He had even labelled himself a confirmed bachelor. He was a serial monogamist at best.

But then again, maybe that was even better. She was full to bursting with the thought of curving one hand through the hair at his nape, of running the other down his broad chest, and of kissing him. She had been sure he had been about to try on the day of the Melbourne Cup, until Jeff had foiled the plan. The mere thought of it raised her body temperature several degrees.

So maybe she should just clear the air, dispel all of that suffocating sexual tension that had settled about the two of them like a cloud heavy with rain. If she threw herself at him, it would get him out of her system. And she knew without a doubt that he would gladly let her go as soon as it was over.

Cara shot a glance his way and wished she hadn't.

He was leaning with one arm propped on the bar, and one foot propped against the bottom rung of a barstool. In his soft navy sweater and tailored tan trousers, he had such casual elegance, such pulsating charisma that even he couldn't keep it in check no matter how hard he tried. And just to top it all off, he was so damn handsome it ached.

And she knew that she could have him without a moment's hesitation. She felt her lungs close up and it took all of her effort to continue to breathe. If she said the word right then, he would ignore the company they had left back at the table and he would take her up to his beautiful hotel suite and he would lead her to his bed and—

'Sorry about the wait, guys,' the heretofore absent bartender said. 'What can I get for you?'

Cara dragged her eyes away and shot the guy a tight smile as she stopped herself from ordering a helpful bucket of iced water.

'Six sparkling apple juices, please.'

'Right! You're the cocktail gang,' the bartender said with a grin. 'Six of the most fabulous-looking sparkling apple juices you have ever seen, coming right up.'

Cara stayed facing the bar, firing up the mantra she had all but forgotten. *Be good. Keep job. Keep home. Anyone and anything not wholly linked to those ideals has to be disregarded unconditionally.*

Adam watched Cara as she watched the bartender. She was wound up tight as a spring. Her high-necked shirt, her tight skirt, her achingly flimsy shoes all supporting the fact that she was wrapping herself up tight inside.

He knew instinctively that beneath Cara's straight-backed outer shell lurked a volcanic heat. He had witnessed moments of it: a quick temper, a determined certainty about her talents, and a ferocious loyalty. And he could not help but wonder if that passion would extend as far as the bedroom. Who was he kidding? He hadn't been idly wondering. For several days now he had been mulling over the idea incessantly. Every time she was in his sight, and every moment she wasn't. This woman was taking him over.

He had to get her out of his system before the wondering became something more deeply ingrained. For a guy who risked ideas and money for a living, that was a risk he could not take.

So, decision made, and timing for once perfect, he leaned

over and whispered in her ear, 'I'm glad to see you're wearing your red shoes again.'

He sensed her control a deep, overwhelming shiver as his whisper tickled at her bare neck. After the moment it took to recover, she glanced down at her shoes, admiring their glossy curves.

'Yes, I am,' she said, her eyes now determinedly fixed on the bartender's back. 'I do tend to buy clothing with the knowledge that it will be worn again and again. I don't have the luxury of being able to use something once and then throw it away.'

Adam knew there was some sort of point she was trying to make but he wasn't totally sure what it was. 'Not many people do.'

'You do.'

That hit him for six. She was angry with him because he had money? That was certainly one to write home about.

'I guess I do have that luxury,' he said carefully. 'But that doesn't mean that I abuse it.'

Finally she turned his way and the inner heat he had been musing over hit him with the blast of an open furnace.

'Really?' she asked, one hand resting on her slim hip. 'You admit you have no trouble throwing people away once you are done with them. So why would you feel any differently about possessions? Some people work their whole lives to make a home for themselves only to have it all slip through their fingers. Most of us can't take it all for granted, you know!'

Her sudden forcefulness shocked him. He reached out and took her by the elbow.

'Hey, come on. What are you going on about?'

'Nothing.'

'Then where is this coming from? What has made you

suddenly so interested in what I do with my things and with the women I date?'

She opened her mouth, ready to breathe fire, but nothing came out. Her green eyes were wide and puzzled. She wasn't angry. She was something else entirely.

He was shocked anew. There was more than plain old heat lurking beneath the surface. She was churning up inside. About him. And not just about his relationships, or his bank balance, but about *him*.

She swallowed hard. Then licked her lips. And he wanted nothing more than to drag her into his arms and kiss away every wild thought that had her so mixed up. He tightened his grip on her arm and she didn't pull away.

'Here you go,' the bartender interrupted cheerfully. 'Six sparkling apple juices.'

The green eyes blinked and shifted away. And the anxiety that seemed ready to swallow her whole seeped slowly away. Adam let go. The moment had passed. In silence they grabbed three drinks each and headed back to the table that was noisy with chatter. But as each of their four companions took a glass the table eased into sudden silence.

Adam dragged his eyes away from Cara to find the others were watching them carefully. They were all smiling, cheekily, and he knew he and Cara weren't fooling anyone. The gang were as aware of the tension between them as he was. But he was pretty sure Cara had not given into the fact yet. She sat down, smoothing out her skirt, fixing her hair, looking anywhere but at him.

'How about a toast?' Gracie said, holding her glass aloft. The others followed suit.

Adam searched desperately for a way to seize Cara's attention. And he found it. He lifted his glass and, harking back to their first lunch together, he said, 'To Cary Grant.'

If only Mr Grant's famous charm could lend him a hand

that night, he would toast him for eternity. It worked. Cara's eyes flickered his way and held. And he read all he needed to know in her tortured gaze.

Gracie broke the searing silence. 'OK... I was thinking more along the lines of: to finding love. But whatever rings your bell. So how about: to Cary Grant *and* finding love?'

Chris grinned and clinked her glass. 'Hear, hear.'

Kelly held one hand to her tummy, her face glowing with a secret smile as she took a sip.

Dean blushed manically as he watched pretty Gracie from over his glass.

And after she had taken a decidedly small sip of her drink, Cara's hands slid to her table, where the pressure she exerted made her knuckles turn white.

Several torturous hours later, Cara listened with half an ear to Gracie and Kelly babbling like a couple of schoolgirls at a slumber party as they trudged back up to her room.

'That was fun,' Gracie said.

'What a nice bunch of guys,' Kelly said. 'That Chris is a sweetheart.'

'Isn't he?' Gracie agreed.

'And Dean had a little thing for you, I think.'

Gracie fluffed a hand in front of her face and became comically coy. 'Oh, he did not.'

'Please,' Kelly insisted. 'He laughed at every joke you made. You're simply not that funny.'

Gracie shrugged. 'Good point.'

'But that Adam is a hard one to figure out,' Kelly said.

Cara flinched, then bit her lip shut tight. There was no response she wished to make to that statement anyway. He twisted her in knots. So what? Nothing was going to come of it. Cara unlocked the door with one swipe of her card and the others followed her inside.

'No, he is not!' Gracie scoffed, flopping down onto Cara's bed. 'He's goo-goo over our classy young friend here.'

'Oh, that much is obvious,' Kelly said, flopping right down beside Gracie. 'The two of them are lit up like floodlights. What I want to know is, why doesn't he darned well do something about it? Because we sure know how stubborn this one is.'

'Hang on a sec,' Gracie said, 'I somehow remember mention of someone she had met before coming in here. The ominous stare, the powerful grace, the serious good looks worthy of a menswear catalogue. That's Adam she was gushing about.'

Cara kept her mouth shut as she slipped out of the shoes and shuffled them into the closet, her unencumbered toes appreciatively scrunching the soft carpet.

'That's it,' Gracie said. 'Both as stubborn as each other, thus doomed from the start. Sitting back in their separate corners, trying so hard to work each other out, when if they were up close and personal the process would be a heck of a lot easier, quicker, and much more fun!'

Cara stood at the end of the bed with her hands on her hips. 'Hello? You two do remember that I am in the room, do you not?'

'Bah!' Gracie said. 'What difference does that make? It's not as though you are going to hear a word we're saying. It's not as though you're going to listen to your brilliant friends. You're going to tuck it all away somewhere safe and quiet and go about the business of buying your big home, keeping yourself to yourself and not turning into your parents.'

'What have they got to do with it?'

'Please!'

'Do you ever wonder why you only date puppy dogs?' Kelly asked, sitting up.

'And lap-dogs at that?' Gracie chimed in. 'Men who do as you say?'

'Because,' Kelly explained, 'you are so darned scared of becoming embroiled in fights the likes of which your parents lived for, you would rather split up than argue.'

Cara could barely hold her ground as the barrage hit her.

Kelly's expression softened but she wasn't done yet. 'Cara, I don't think that big hunk of man out there would be the type to follow you around saying "yes, dear, no, dear, three bags full, dear". By the look on his face all night it looked like he was more than ready to give you some very specific instructions and if you aren't prepared to follow them, look out!'

Cara rolled her shoulders, easing out the rising tension. And then she stopped halfway. She was doing exactly what the girls were saying she always did. Preparing herself to moderate, negotiate, anything to bring about peace. Anything to stop the fight.

'OK. What if I agree that you're right?'

Kelly opened her mouth to say, I told you so, but Cara held up a hand to stop her.

'I am the queen negotiator. Always the diplomat. Fine. So be it. But this has nothing to do with my relationship with Adam.'

'Your relationship?'

Cara threw out her arms in exasperation. 'My friendship, my acquaintance, whatever you want to call it! We've been thrown together a good deal during the filming of the show, but that's all. Circumstances have pushed us together, nothing else. We might have developed an…attraction of sorts, but that's it. Certainly nothing to hang your hopes on.'

Kelly and Gracie sat on the bed staring at Cara, wearing matching grins on their faces.

Gracie broke the silence. 'I doth thinkest she doth protesteth too much.'

Cara grabbed a couple of cushions off her small couch and dived on the bed, doing her best to smother the cheeky grins from both friends' faces.

'So what's with you and Miss Cat's Eyes?' Dean asked as Adam and Chris walked him to his car.

Adam shot Chris a look but he held up his hands in surrender. 'Don't look at me. I've not said a word.'

'So there is something going on?' Dean asked.

'No. There most definitely is not.'

'Please!' Dean shot back. 'I've never seen you so withdrawn. I almost felt the need to poke you once or twice to see if you were still with us, while she fidgeted like she had fleas.'

'I'm amazed you could see anything past the impertinent brunette at your side.'

Dean's ears grew red instantly.

'Hey, don't change the subject,' Chris insisted. 'The whole problem is that nothing has been happening but he would like nothing more than for there to be lots happening. He's been impossible since the day he met her.'

'Which also happens to be the same day you told me about this show of yours,' Adam reminded him.

They reached Dean's car and Chris leapt on Adam, putting him in a head lock. 'Come on, Deano,' Chris said. 'Between the two of us we might be able to lock him in the trunk of the car and you can keep him away from me for the duration.'

'I'm not going anywhere,' Adam insisted, twisting easily away from his slighter friend.

'And why not? What are you achieving by being here? The show is almost finished, so you can't stop it now. Especially now you've seen the projections of the exposure it will give us. I win. I was right. The ideas man got it right. What a shock. So why stay?'

'Moral support.'

'Pfft. What? You'll miss my moral support of you?'

'Fine. Then let's call it unfinished business.'

'Between you and Cara, right?'

His friends watched him with bright eyes. They were smart guys and he could deny it all night long, but they wouldn't believe it for a second.

So he afforded them one short nod.

'That's more like it!' Dean said, giving Chris a sly low five. 'Wow, you guys are making me antsy. I feel like I'm missing out on something big.' Dean hopped into the driver's seat of his sporty number. 'I'll see you guys next week, right?'

'Three more days and this will all be over,' Chris said, his voice suddenly heavy with exhaustion.

'And has it been worth it?' Dean asked.

Adam watched from the sidelines as his friend's face lit up.

'More than I could have ever hoped.'

Adam knew without a doubt his friend was in love. Though the main reason why Adam had kept so close to Chris this whole time had been to make sure that he would be safe from the clutches of any of these women, Chris had fallen and he had fallen hard.

Adam was too late. He had failed. So why didn't he feel as torn up about the fact as he should?

Cara walked the girls downstairs and saw them off in the lobby. They waved frantically all the way through the revolving doors and Cara watched as their sprightly forms shimmied into a wavering mirage and disappeared.

Then through the doors came Adam, head down, hands in pockets, walking slowly, his attention a million miles away. He hadn't noticed her, and if she headed for the stairs they would not cross paths. But her slipper-clad feet were rooted to the spot.

Kelly was right; he lit her up. He made her think, he made her reconsider her opinions, and he made her want to fight back. And rather than having the battle eat away at her until she didn't know any other way to communicate, she felt all the more alive for it.

He was simply in an altogether different league from any guy she had ever known. Even from the producers who earned enough dough to wear comparable clothes. But he wore them better, he wore them as if he were born into them. Where others stood, he lounged. They spoke, he drawled. He was just the most attractive, disturbing man Cara had ever known.

When he was only a few steps from her, Adam looked up. She knew the moment he spied her. The perpetually crinkled brow smoothed away, and he smiled. His pace picked up and he stood straighter. It amazed her that she could bring about such a sudden change in the demeanour of a guy like him.

'Beautiful night for it,' he said as he approached.

'Mmm?' she said, flinching at his unexpected words.

A beautiful night for what? For falling for someone who would never have you? For putting yourself through growing torment just for one more moment in someone's precious company? For mad, debilitating terror that you were falling prey to something that would change you for ever?

'Beautiful night,' Cara agreed.

Adam shot her a sweet smile and she hoped she smiled

back, though it felt more like a panic-riddled grimace. Then as he came closer he looked to her feet and spied her slippers. His glance shifted back to hers, his beautiful eyes questioning but still smiling and creating the most wonderful tumbling sensation in her stomach.

What could she do? She was undone. The girls were right. She'd had enough of yes-men. She wanted a real man.

The moment that she had missed by the pool and the moment that had been stolen from her at the races were not moments she could live with missing entirely. She had insisted that Chris have no regrets in his life; it was only fair that she do as she preached.

So in the quiet, air-conditioned stillness of the hotel lobby at midnight, Cara took the final two slipper-clad steps and threw herself into Adam's arms, kissing him with every ounce of passion she harboured, as it would have to be her only chance.

Adam stiffened for only a brief, stunned moment before his strong arms wrapped her tight. This man spoke only when he had something important to say and his kisses held the same authority. Cara knew she was being treated to something special. Something significant. His indulgent, hot-blooded kiss told her he had longed for this just as much as she had.

Cara instantly buried her hands deep within his soft hair, as she had wanted to do since the first moment she'd laid eyes on him. She could feel the hardness of his chest through the softness of his expensive navy sweater, the fabric rubbing along her inner arms, the smooth sensation enough to make her melt her whole body against his. She delighted in the knowledge that his curves fitted against hers as though he had been carved just for her.

Waves of finally unbridled need crashed down on her

and she lost herself in Adam's luscious kiss as she never
had lost herself before. Cara's head felt light and empty.
She would have happily endured the exquisite kiss until it
sapped away her last breath. But as though sensing her
imminent collapse Adam pulled away, ever so slightly, the
heat not easing but shifting, slowing, burning slower and
hotter still, so that now she could take the time to experience every nuance, every variance, every sensation he afforded her.

Her whole body ached as it craved ever more. It flushed
from his desire, his skill, his reverence. She was so im-
mersed in the kiss, Cara's lungs felt ready to collapse. She
had to take a breath. Though she felt willing to drown in
the warmth of his lips, her lungs made the decision for her.

She pulled away, raking in great gulping breaths of air
so cold it ached.

Adam looked down into Cara's wild eyes. Her pupils
were dilated, the glittering colour surrounding them deep
and mysterious as emeralds. He leant in and placed a kiss
on the end of her nose. He felt so much tenderness towards
her in that moment it physically hurt. Endorphins whipped
through his entire body, both relaxing and invigorating
every part of him. And his chest ached, as though he was
using muscles within that he had never used before.

'We shouldn't be doing this here,' Cara whispered, drawing Adam back to the present.

Adam was infinitely glad she had added the word 'here'.
'There is nobody about,' he said, his voice eloquently
husky. 'Everyone else is in bed.'

That word was enough for their combined temperature
to rise. He could feel her heart beating through his chest,
her beautiful, kind, heavily protected heart. But Adam felt
her pull away, physically and emotionally. No! He wasn't
about to let her kiss him like that and then retreat. He

dragged her back into his embrace but she would no longer look him in the eye.

'I can't do this,' she said.

'And why is that?' he asked, running a hand up and down her straight back. He felt her shiver in his arms, the reaction flowing through him as well.

'Because working relationships amount to trouble. And this job is really important to me. It's a career maker and I can't let anything stand in the way of that.'

'From what I've heard you had a pretty darned good career to start with.'

She shook her head, refusing to listen to reason. 'I will not jeopardise this job to indulge myself with some sort of holiday romance. This may feel like a walk in the park for you, a bit of relax time away from the office, but this is it for me. This is a career clincher. This job means more to me than you can know. So don't make me blow it.'

She looked up at him then and her internal struggle shook him. It wasn't that she couldn't go to the next step with him, it was that she desperately wished she didn't want to.

'How can I make you do anything?' he asked.

'By looking at me like that. All sure and dark and brooding and strong and lovely and…'

He sensed her winding down as she went, as though with each word her desire became too much, piling up on itself, growing exponentially with every reason why she was attracted to him. Her words speaking less truth to him than her body, he leaned down to take up where they'd left off but she turned away at the last second.

'What's going on? You were the one who kissed me just now,' he said, knowing it was a low blow. But he couldn't help it. His body was singing and he couldn't fathom why she would even want to fight it. Or even how she had the physical strength to do so, because he sure didn't.

She swallowed. Hard. 'So I was. And that was wrong of me so I apologise. But that has to be the end of it. That has to be enough.'

It wasn't. Not nearly. But Adam was not one to push a woman past 'no'.

'Fine,' he said, his frustration making the word explode from his mouth. Something inside him wrenched as he saw the intense relief wash across her face and he knew in that moment that if he had decided to push past 'no' there would have been no further resistance.

But then he also knew that she would have hated him and herself in the morning and though that once would not have concerned him, with her it did.

'Come on,' he said, his voice deliberately sympathetic. He held out a hand, shepherding her towards the open lift.

Low on resistance, she fell into step beside him. She didn't look his way and he didn't make her. He felt the abyss at his toes once more and the only thing holding him from falling was the most tenuous of reasons.

His greatest fear had been realised: that one kiss would never be enough. Now that he had tasted of her sweetness, he wanted more. He had to have more. Especially since it seemed it would be the only way to rid himself of the caving ache that had gradually taken up residence in the pit of his stomach.

Her kisses were honest, even if she was not. He knew she wanted more from him than one stolen kiss even if she could not admit it aloud.

The lift stopped on her floor. He led her to her room and when she couldn't for the life of her get the key card to work he took it from her trembling hand and unlocked the door for her.

She took a step inside the room, turned and faced him, her cheek leaning against the edge of the door.

The carpet in the hallway was different from the carpet in the room, the line where they joined taking on one hell of a significance. If he took that one step across that line, they would spend the night in each other's arms. If he kept himself on this side of that line, they could look each other in the eye in the morning.

The decision was suddenly easy. It was more important for her to like him than for him to seduce her. Not to help Chris. Not for the good of the company. But for him.

'Goodnight, Cara,' he said. 'Sweet dreams.'

Taking in a deep breath gave him the time to imprint her sweet, sleepy face on his memory. But that alone was one step too far. Before he could stop himself he took the leap into the abyss.

'I'm in Suite 45,' he said.

Cara's eyes flared with suppressed desire. Her lips disappeared as she bit down on them hard.

'Goodnight, Adam,' she said, her husky voice wafting over him like the caress it was.

And as Cara closed the door to her room Adam's whole body vibrated with the most intense, unresolved sensations he had ever experienced.

CHAPTER TEN

LYING in bed, still wide awake an hour later, Cara thought back to the promise she had made to the good fairies right back at the beginning of her adventure. If she landed the job, she would never want for anything else.

Her wish had been granted but she was not keeping up her side of the bargain. She had become greedy with her success. Her real potential was opening up before her as never before. She wanted the job and she wanted more. And she wanted it with Adam.

Gracie would tell her it was the age of safe sex. But Cara knew that sex would never be safe with Adam. To her, 'safe' also meant that she would come out of the episode unscathed. If she let herself be led into Adam's waiting arms, she would be anything but safe. She would be lost. And once gone, she did not know if she would have the strength to find herself again. For a girl who had done it alone for almost ten years, the thought was terrifying.

Cara all but fell out of bed as a loud knock sounded at her door.

Adam's sensuous voice saying the overloaded words, 'I'm in Suite 45,' reverberated with each of the continuing knocks.

Cara grabbed her delicate nightgown and wrapped it about her, looping the tie in a triple knot around her waist.

She opened the door, her expectant face switching to shock in an instant as Kelly's husband stood before her.

'Simon! What are you doing here? It's one o'clock in the morning!' She whipped her head around the corner, finding the usually bustling hallway magically devoid of crew. 'Besides which, if I'm seen talking to you I'll be sacked.'

Simon stuck his foot in the door so she couldn't close it. Cara looked up at him in bewilderment.

'Cara, it's Gracie.'

She no longer needed Simon's foot for the door to remain wide open. She was out in the hallway in a heartbeat. 'What? What happened?'

'It's her mother. This evening, in Sydney… Gracie's mother has been killed in a car crash.'

It took Cara half a second before she was off down the hallway to Jeff's room. She banged on the door until Jeff finally appeared looking as bedraggled as always. 'Do you have any idea what time it is?'

'I've just had some bad news. A friend of mine has had some bad news and I have to go to her.'

Jeff shook his head and yawned. 'Sorry, Cara. Can't let you go. There's only another three days left of the shoot. Wait until then.'

'Come on, buddy,' Simon said, appearing at Cara's side, 'don't do this to her.'

That brought Jeff awake like a slap to the face. 'Who is this?'

'This is Simon. Another friend. He came to tell me the bad news.'

'How did you get in here?' Jeff asked, all five feet eight of him trying to outmuscle the much bigger Simon, and all five feet eight failing miserably.

'That doesn't matter,' Simon said. 'What matters is I'm taking her home with me now.'

Jeff's eyes narrowed. 'Fine. But if you do she's not coming back. If you go, Cara, you will have broken your contract and we don't have to pay you a red cent.'

Maya's words tumbled through her mind. *TV jobs are notoriously precarious. Don't cause trouble. Do your job with a minimum of fuss and you'll be fine.* Having a stranger at Jeff's door so late at night while wearing nothing but a nightgown would not be classed as a minimum of fuss in anyone's book.

'Jeff, you're not shooting until this evening. I'll be back by then, I promise.'

'Sorry,' Jeff said. 'Just wait the three days and you're free as a bird.'

Cara stared through him, biting on her lip as her mind whirled with the pile-up of bad news blocking her way to a clear decision.

Then she turned and ran. She wrenched open the stairwell door and took the steps two at a time, not even waiting to check if Simon was on her tail. When she reached the next floor she went straight to Suite 45. She banged on the door. Adam appeared, still wearing the same clothes he had been in at dinner.

Adam took in Cara's attire. No matter his brazen invitation, he had never actually expected her to come knocking, especially decked out in such seriously gorgeous get up.

Her gown had slipped open, the tie dragging along behind her. Her hair was wild and curling about her face. And she huffed and puffed, her chest rising and falling as though she had run all the way to his room. He had never seen anything so sexy in all his life.

His body responded in an instant. He could feel a low growl of desire welling from within and he knew how the cavemen felt. He wanted nothing more than to reach out, grab a hold and drag her into his cave.

But only then was he able to see past his own desire to

the state she was in. She wasn't panting at his door in response to his invitation. Something was wrong.

He reached out and took her by the arm, his grip purposefully gentle.

'Sweetheart, what is it?'

'I've never asked anything of you before, and I wouldn't now if it wasn't an emergency, but you are my last hope. You have to convince Jeff to let me go.' Her voice was ragged and her eyes wild, the green flecks flashing. 'He won't and I have to and he says that I can't leave or he'll renege on the contract and he can't. I need that money. But if he does I'll go anyway. But I was hoping you could help.'

'Help what, sweetheart?' he asked, pulling the poor haggard girl into a soothing embrace. Anything to stop her from quaking. He couldn't stand watching her look so frightened.

'It's Gracie. You met Gracie.'

'I met Gracie,' he agreed, running one hand up and down her slender back, the silky fabric rising and falling through his fingers.

'Her mother...'

She stopped and he could feel her gulping down a breath.

'Her mother has just been killed on holiday in Sydney. Her stepfather is up there, and she never knew her real father, so she needs me. And there is no way that I am going to leave her alone tonight. There is just no way.'

'Of course you're not.'

Adam looked up the hallway to see a man he did not know striding towards them. Thinking the big guy was a security guard, he whipped Cara around behind him, putting his own bulk between her and any trouble.

'Cara?' the man said as he approached, and Adam knew

by the care in his voice that this was no security guard. This guy knew her. But still, Adam kept her shielded.

'What can I do for you, mate?' Adam asked, his voice coming out so low and ominous it surprised even him.

'I'm Simon. A friend of Cara's. Kelly's husband.'

At that news Adam relaxed immeasurably. Suddenly he had himself an ally, not a challenger. He put the thought of what that meant from his mind. There were more important things to do before that could even hope to be tackled.

'Great,' Adam said. 'Take her back to her room for me and help her get what she needs. Then have her downstairs in fifteen minutes. OK?'

Simon paused for a brief moment and Adam knew he was being sized up. They were like two stags looking out for the same doe, though he knew instinctively that their motives were very different.

Obviously getting all he needed from Adam's silent entreaty, Simon gave him one curt nod, then took Cara by the hand and, with one arm wrapped about her slim shoulders, herded her to the lift.

Adam whipped inside his room long enough to grab his key card, then he headed off to do what he had to do.

Fifteen minutes later Cara was in a limousine heading back to St Kilda Storeys. Simon sat next to her, watching over her like a protective older brother as she stayed on the phone with Kelly the whole way. Kelly, who was at Gracie's side back home.

As they pulled into the driveway Cara had the same view of her home as she'd had less than two weeks before. But rather than coming home and running up and hugging the warm stucco that belonged to her, and her alone, her heart ached with the knowledge that she would have to wait a good while longer.

But no matter.

Though it shocked the hell out of her to realise it, there were more important things in her life than a pile of bricks. And one of those things was upstairs nursing a broken heart.

Simon opened the door and went to the back of the car to get her luggage. Then as Cara stepped out she smacked into the large frame of Adam Tyler.

Momentarily forgetting where she was and what she was doing there, she simply stared into his big blue eyes.

'I…I was up front,' he said, his voice quiet and uncertain. 'I didn't want to crowd you. But before I head off I wanted to make sure you were going to be OK.'

'I'll see you upstairs,' Simon said and Cara followed his voice. She saw the brief nods that Adam and Simon shared, then realised that Adam had done this all for her. He had organised the car. He was under the same contractual stranglehold she was, and likely had a hell of a lot more to lose from the deal than a few thousand dollars, yet he had left the hotel to make sure she was all right. She had asked for help and without argument he had come through for her. He had put in danger his company's position with the station to help her.

The moonlight created a halo of light around his beautiful face and she found herself reaching out and taking a hold of his large hand and saying, 'Please don't go. Not yet.'

They stood like that for a few moments. He finally gave her hand a quick squeeze, then let go and bent to chat to the driver. Cara saw the light on in Gracie's top-floor window. With a deep ragged breath she headed up to her friend, feeling secure in the knowledge that Adam was right behind her, supporting her all the way.

She opened the unlocked door to Gracie's apartment and, by the look of pure relief on her friend's red face, she knew without a doubt she had made the right decision. Cara ran to her best friend, and card-carrying member of her urban family, and wrapped her tight.

Hours later Adam stretched out his neck as he filled the kettle in Cara's downstairs apartment.

Cara came back from the bathroom where she had gone to splash cold water on her tired face. She then flopped into the large leather sofa with all the coordination of a rag doll and remained where she landed, lying across the couch, one leg dangling onto the floor and one arm flung across her tired eyes. She looked so small. But hours of hugging and consoling a devastated best friend could do that to a person.

Through the night, Adam had witnessed exactly the sort of emotional involvement he had sought to avoid in trying to talk Chris out of this whole escapade in the first place. He had seen his father rise and fall with the women in his life so many times that he had come to the conclusion that any such grief and loss was self-inflicted. It was simple. *Don't care and you won't find cause to grieve.*

But when Cara had asked him to stay, the thought of simply not caring had been inconceivable. And even when the tears had been flying thick and fast in Gracie's apartment upstairs he had not been able to drag himself away. The desire to be there if Cara needed him had been stronger than the desire to shield himself from the potency of the enshrouding emotions. It had been quite a night.

Once the kettle was boiled he poured a cup of black instant coffee for himself and a sweet white for Cara. He carried the cups over, resting them on the big wooden coffee-table as gently as he could as he sat in the chair opposite hers. But the smell must have reached her just the same.

'Mmm,' she said, her arm shifting just enough to reveal her lovely eyes, which blinked slowly, sleepily, at him.

He couldn't move. He was frozen in time, mesmerised by that lush mouth of hers curling into a slow, appreciative smile. Then she stretched, her whole lithe body yielding and unwinding before him. Finally her face erupted into a great gaping yawn and she pulled herself into a sitting position. Blinking sleepily at him some more, she grinned.

'What are you grinning at?' he asked and sat back, enjoying her first smile all night.

'I feel like I'm playing hookey,' she whispered.

'Private school girl, hey?'

'Yep.'

'Were your parents doctors or lawyers?'

She shook her head vehemently. 'Good Lord. Neither. Scholarships all the way for me.'

'So you were a brainiac.'

Her eyes smiled at him from over her mug of coffee, their emerald depths glistening back at him.

'And you weren't?'

He shrugged. 'I did well enough. So why didn't you become a doctor or a lawyer? Can't stand the sight of blood?'

That earned him another grin and he found he was amassing quite a collection of them, and they were that good he had the feeling he would be keeping them with him to bring out on cold, lonely nights.

'Oh, I like action well enough. There's plenty of bloodshed in my business but at least there I am the decision maker; I'm the end of the line. What I say goes. I brook no arguments, or I walk.'

'I saw that tonight. When I happened on Jeff he looked

like he didn't know what hit him. He must have thought he'd bought himself a lap-dog when he took you on.'

'Then he didn't do as much research as he originally professed.'

Adam nodded. The conversation had hit a natural lull and for several moments they sipped on their coffees, simply enjoying each other's company. He watched as Cara tucked her feet beneath her, shuffling her bottom until she was comfortable, her slight frame sinking happily into the large seat.

Adam glanced around the apartment. It was stylish and homey at the same time. Cosy. Comfortable. 'I like your place.'

Cara followed his gaze and he saw her face light up again but the brightness diminished as though someone had snuffed out a burning candle.

'Me too. It's almost all mine, you know. The whole building.'

'I'm impressed. You did it without having to be a doctor or a lawyer...'

'Or part-owner in a multibillion-dollar company,' they said in tandem.

Adam could not believe he was making jokes about money with a woman. It was just surreal.

She nodded, her mouth twisting as she bit at her lower lip. Adam knew this meant she was disconcerted. By now he knew what pretty much all of her little idiosyncratic expressions meant. It wasn't as though he had purposely studied them, they were just that memorable, and just so particular to her.

OK, so he had studied them too.

'With this job I could have paid it off. But now I have run out on the production...' She finished off on an expressive shrug.

He remembered her saying in amongst her earlier ramblings in the hotel how important this pay-cheque was to her. And then for the first time in his life he found himself uttering the words, 'If you need the money—'

Cara held up her hands, stopping his words short. 'Don't even think it, Adam. There is nothing more likely to ruin a relationship than money.'

And he was so relieved at her words he wanted to throw himself into her arms and bury his face in her warmth and never let go.

It was enough to have him leap to his feet and ask, 'How about breakfast?'

Adam looked suddenly lost. As though he didn't know what to do with his hands. Cara figured he had every right to be antsy. He'd put up with a lot that night, more than she would have expected of anyone. Even Kelly and Simon had headed home some time after three. Yet Adam had stayed.

Cara glanced at the closed pantry doors, imagining the delights within. 'It'll have to be cornflakes or two-week-old eggs, I'm afraid.'

'Sit,' Adam insisted. 'Stay here. I'm going out for a walk and I'll bring something back.'

Cara nodded. He wanted to leave. He needed fresh air. But she didn't blame him. He hadn't asked for this. Hadn't asked for a night comforting practical strangers. If he had reached his limit she couldn't blame him at all.

He didn't even turn at the door when he left. She wouldn't be surprised if he didn't come back, if he made some excuse and ran for his life. And though she tried to pretend she was OK with the thought, it sapped the last of her resolve. She slumped back into her soft couch, the last remnants of her energy finally leaving her as tranquil, heavenly sleep took her over.

*   *   *

The smell of store-bought coffee laced with cinnamon invaded her senses. And croissants. And jam. And something else... She sniffed the air and peeled open an eye.

Adam was back. She could see him silhouetted against a wash of morning sun streaming through the small side window. Her heart grew so that she could barely breathe.

On the dining table she saw the something else. A huge bunch of fresh flowers took pride of place as a centre-piece. Adam had obviously not been able to find a vase so they resided in an unused spaghetti canister. Daisies, her favourite flower. The same scent as her favoured perfume. She had a feeling he knew it, too.

Cara sat up and only when Adam turned her way did she realise the creaking groan she had just heard had come from her.

'Good morning, sunshine,' he said.

Cara ran a hand through her tumble of short curls. 'How long have you been gone?' she asked, hiding the burgeoning tenderness from her voice under the mask of a yawn.

'Half an hour at most.'

'Are you sure it's not really tomorrow?'

He raised an eyebrow.

'Are you sure I haven't just had the most delicious, rejuvenating twenty-four-hour sleep?'

A smile kicked at the side of his mouth. 'Pretty sure. Sorry.'

Cara peeled herself from the chair, her joints aching, her whole body heavy with exhaustion, and her heart singing that he had returned to her. She realised Adam must have felt pretty much just as achy and exhausted, but instead of hotfooting it back to the hotel for a couple of hours of much-needed sleep, or running for the hills and out of her life altogether, he had returned to her with flowers and breakfast.

Her heart ached with the perfection of the scene: the mouth-watering display of croissants, muffins, pancakes, sausages and eggs, the thoughtful flowers, a man she adored seated at the head of the table. She had to take the edge off before she burst into tears.

'Wow!' she exclaimed merrily as she sat.

'What?'

'Are we having company?'

'Not that I know of.'

'Do I look like the sort of girl who can wolf this lot down?' With that, Cara's tummy let out a groan to match any in history. She couldn't help but laugh. 'OK. So maybe I am just that sort of girl. Load me up a plate.'

'All I ask is that you leave me a bite.'

She shot him a smile, feeling warm and fuzzy with tiredness. 'We'll see.'

Adam filled up Cara's plate as asked. He was famished and he could tell she was too. So only once she was satisfied did he take a seat and grab some food for himself.

'What do you think Gracie will do now?' he asked.

Cara looked up at her ceiling as though curling out her thoughts to her friend a few floors above.

'I really don't know. Her mother became pregnant with Gracie when she was in her late teens. Gracie never knew her father. I don't think he's even Australian. And her mother married Gracie's stepfather when she—Gracie— was in high school, so her half-siblings are still pretty young. Her stepdad's a lovely guy, so I'm sure if Gracie decided to go and stay with him and her half-brother and sister that would be fine.'

'But will she? She doesn't seem the type to lean on people too easily.'

'She's not.'

'Which is why you had to come. You knew she would lean on you. Her urban family.'

'Exactly.' An amazed smile grew on her face and it kicked at something deep inside him. 'You are too astute for your own good.'

'It comes in handy.'

'In your work, sure. But it must be hard to give people a second go if you know that your first impressions are usually so bang on.'

Cara smiled up at him and he couldn't for the life him remember what she had just said. She was all warm and rumpled with sleep. Her cheeks were pink, her hair ruffled and curling about her face, which was long since devoid of make-up. Her smattering of freckles stood out on her sweet nose.

She must have thought she had not explained herself well enough so she rephrased her question.

'I mean, if someone makes a bad first impression, how could you ever trust them again?'

She shook her head sadly, then tucked into her breakfast and Adam relaxed once he realised that her conversation had become rhetorical. He was thankful when they settled into a companionable silence.

It was halfway through the meal before Adam wondered how long it had been since he had eaten breakfast in companionable silence with anyone.

His rare breakfasts with his father were anything but companionable. They were always fraught with disappointment on Adam's side, and resentment from his father that he'd had to fall back onto his son's fortune since losing all of his own.

And breakfasts with Chris or Dean were anything but silent. They were always noisy and energetic as the three of them sparred back and forth with new ideas.

But this breakfast experience was new to him. It was leisurely, it was peaceful and it was pleasant. And to add to the conundrum, he was eating this delicious, companionable, comfortably silent breakfast with a woman. He could not recall a time when that had ever happened.

He watched Cara from beneath his lashes. Her gaze was aimed towards the window, but, with nothing more interesting in her path than the neighbour's garage wall, he knew her mind was far away. She bit into her croissant vacantly, chewed slowly, her wide green eyes blinking slowly into the sun.

Without warning she turned his way and he was caught staring. She sent him a warm sweet smile that spoke of comfort and sunshine and all things nice.

His heart flipped in his chest.

Again she had blessed him with a moment of simple joy that he did not want to ever forget. In fact this was a moment he did not want to have happen only once in his lifetime. He wanted to experience again and again. And not just with anyone.

But with her.

CHAPTER ELEVEN

'SO YOU only date puppy dogs?' Adam said out of the blue.

Cara blinked and drew her attention from her daydreams to the man who had been featuring in them. *Where had that statement come from?* she wondered. But then, when her sleepy focus snapped back into place, she knew. There was more than just friendly interest in his eyes.

In an instant her heart rate doubled, and, for someone who saw exercise as something other people did, she felt that doubled heart rate in every limb.

'And you only date brainless bimbos,' she lobbed back, her voice unfortunately heavy and languorous.

The twinkle in his eyes showed he knew just how he affected her. 'And so far how do you think that has worked for the both of us?'

She slowly lowered her fork, her gaze unable to disentangle from his. 'Not so well, obviously,' she admitted. 'Or else we would both be settled with toddlers scampering about our feet by now.'

He nodded. Slowly. 'Maybe it's time we break the mould. Try something new.'

Was he saying what she thought he was saying? Was the gorgeous, emotionally unavailable, confirmed bachelor, billionaire Adam Tyler saying that he would like for them to try each other on for size?

If Cara had felt the double heart rate in every limb, the shortness of breath that suddenly hit her like a sack of flour to the chest was a whole other sensation. The brick in her chest that she had felt for so long was nothing in comparison. She gripped a hold of the edge of the dining table so as not to swoon from her chair.

Adam watched her with his usual quiet patience. Well, he would have to wait. Her answer would be one of the most important of her life.

Think, Cara. Think!

Gorgeous—God, yes.

Emotionally unavailable—surely as much as ever. But aren't you the same?

Confirmed bachelor—meaning he would never try to change you so as to keep you. Isn't that perfect?

Billionaire.

That was where it all fell apart. Money ruined everything. Her parents hadn't had enough to keep them happy. But since then she had seen where too much could cause just as many squabbles and levels of mistrust. Adam was as damaged as she was by his parents' failings, and that was the last thing she needed to be reminded of every day.

Relax! This is no marriage proposal. He is not asking you to move to the other side of the world and become his love slave. He has just thrown out the idea that two consenting adults who find each other appealing might want to consider the idea of dating.

Who was she kidding? They didn't just find each other *appealing*, the two of them could run a small town on the electricity they produced between them, so any sort of affair would be…unforgettable.

But then she knew. It would not only be unforgettable, it would be unbeatable. If she ever had Adam, she did not think that any other relationship would compare.

Along with the face Adam presented to the world was the Adam she had come to know over the last several days. He was extraordinarily perceptive, doggedly loyal, and infinitely lovable. So he wore suits that cost ten times as much as her one pair of Kate Madden Designs shoes, but he didn't flaunt his money in any way that she had seen. He used his powers for good, to look after a friend in need, to give some exercise and sunshine to a group of virtual strangers whom he thought might like it, and she had no idea who or what he had threatened to get her out of the hotel the night before and to Gracie as quickly as he had.

And the fact that he didn't speak unless he had something to say just showed what a good listener he was. Cara had not had too much experience with people who actually listened. Her parents had screamed their opinions at one another without ever answering one another's questions. Any way she looked at it, he was a good man.

The fact of the matter was, she had fallen deeply and longingly in love with him. So, contrarily, the answer had to be no.

No matter how much he seemed to care for her, he had never given her any indication that his thoughts on long-term relationships were anything other than exactly as his biography suggested. And any sort of dalliance with him would be so unforgettable she could very well not get over it. It would be unforgettable and bust.

She peeled her fingers from the table and sat forward, her answer fixed. 'Or maybe we stick to our guns so as not to fall prey to outside forces telling us what they think our lives should be like.'

He did his blinking thing. 'There is always that argument.'

Cara took the several beats of silence to meditate her beating heart to a more manageable pace.

'So how has it been working for you?' he asked.

'Hmm?'

'Sticking to your guns.'

Pretty well. Fantastically. I love my life.

Those were all perfectly reasonable responses to his question. But Cara knew in that moment that they were not true.

Her life was nice. Busy. Ordered. But that was hardly the message she wanted written on her tombstone. Outrageous. Hectic. Abundant with love. Now those were descriptions to be proud of.

She looked up to find Adam watching her. He was nodding.

'Yep,' he agreed, though she had not said a word out loud. 'I thought as much.'

'Did you now?'

'I did. Because it's pretty much the same for me.'

Cara knew they were talking in circles and she knew what they were talking in circles about. But though Adam was doing his thing, leaving big great gaping holes for her to fill, she could not drag the words from her mouth. Instead she bit at her bottom lip.

'You do that a lot, you know.'

'Hmm?'

He leaned over and, taking a hold of her chin, ran his thumb over her bottom lip, which grew soft and pliant in his caress. 'You nibble at your bottom lip.' His hand pulled away.

'I used to suck my thumb as a kid and since I stopped it has become a sort of makeshift habit.' Cara's hand reached up to rub away the tingles Adam's thumb had left behind.

'Mmm. And there I was thinking that you do it especially when you're holding something back.'

Of course she did. And of course he would know it too.

'You don't have to hold back, you know,' he offered. 'Whatever you have to say, I can take it.'

Cara ached to drag her lip between her teeth. 'You're one to talk,' she said.

Adam laughed, a low rumbling sound that Cara felt in the pit of her stomach.

'You have a point there,' he said. 'It seems we are two very similar creatures, Cara. Obstinate. Opinionated. Closed to possibilities that we might be wrong.'

'Well, I guess there's no hope for us, then, is there?'

Cara knew he could have taken it one of two ways. That there was no hope that either of them would ever really change, or that there was no hope for the two of them to come together. Either way she felt she had made her point. He had asked her not to hold back, and that was as close as she could come to telling it as it was without hurting herself or him.

She waited for his response.

Would he sigh and say, *I guess you're right?* Or would he stare deep into her eyes and promise to show her how wrong she was? The longer it took for him to reply, the harder Cara found it to breathe. And the more she hoped it would be the second response.

By the time Adam cleared his throat Cara was so stiff with concern she flinched. She looked into his deep dark blue eyes to find them glancing over her face with concern, and with a modicum of humour. A tolerant smile had settled upon his face.

'There's always hope.'

He stood up and began clearing the plates and when he reached her side he bent to place a soft kiss atop her head. She bit her lip so hard she drew blood. But she had no choice. She had to stop herself from throwing herself into his dish-laden arms and letting him know the extent of her secret hopes.

* * *

Later that morning Adam helped her from the limo. As they looked up at the beautiful façade of the hotel it looked more like a fortress than ever.

'Are you sure you want to go in there alone?' Adam asked. His guiding hand resting softly at her back felt so like a brand.

'Absolutely,' Cara said on an outward breath.

'You do realise Jeff is going to eat you alive. Beneath all that strange hair lives a real-life television executive and a more ferocious beast you will never hope to meet.'

'Even so.'

As they entered the lift together Cara realised that the job did not mean to her what it once had. There was something more important in her life. Something that had always been there, but only after last night had she realised how important it was.

Friendship. The people in her life were bigger than the things in her life. If she had nothing, if for some reason she lost St Kilda Storeys, Kelly, Gracie and, yes, even her beloved Adam would take her in and give her the shelter she'd thought she so desperately needed. She waited for that same old sunken feeling to take up residence in her chest, but it never came. A smile eased across her tired face.

So her parents had fought. So her father had not earned enough money to keep her mother happy. So her mother had spent too much money to keep her father happy. They had had each other. That was why they'd stayed together through the lean years and through the fights. They had known that having each other was more important than anything else. To them love had been enough.

As they readied to part ways, Cara ached to prolong their time alone together. 'Thanks again for last night,' she said.

'Any time.'

She leaned in and gave him a thankful kiss on the cheek. She could not help herself. It hardly rated against their impassioned clinch the night before but she still felt blessed to be able to feel his warm cheek against her own.

With a deep intake of breath Adam turned and left her on her own. Cara knocked.

'I could fire you, you know,' Jeff said, hanging up his mobile phone as he opened the door. Cara almost laughed. His hair was spikier than she had ever seen it. It was almost a parody of itself.

'There is nothing to smile about here, Cara. You broke our contracted agreement. And as such I could kick you out on your bony ass without paying you a cent.'

She waited for the cold lick of fear to take her by the throat but it didn't come. Realising that in the grand scheme of things it did not matter made her feel free. She felt peace wash over her. She would pay off her building. Maybe not this month. Maybe not this year. But she would get there. By her own blood, sweat and tears, her own late nights and weekends, she would do it.

Besides, she had long since proven she was not built to keep her head down and be good.

'So fire me,' Cara said, eyeing him levelly, and enjoying immensely the look of utter shock on his young face.

He coughed and spluttered and sought meaner words until Cara cut him off.

'Just hold up there, Jeff. You know I want this gig, or else I wouldn't have gone after it. I want the exposure that will come from having my name on the credits. And, yes, I want the pay-cheque. But I am the best damn stylist in town. I am highly sought after, I am paid well, and I am as good as it gets. So keep me, don't keep me. It's up to you. Keep me so that on the final episode your bachelor, who adores me as I adore him, and would be pretty miffed to know I have been treated badly, will look better than you have ever seen him. Or let me go and see how your precious show turns out without me.'

Jeff stared her down, but the wind had well and truly gone from his sails. 'Well, actually, I have just been talking with the station manager and we have decided that your leave of absence was understandable and we would like to keep you on. With full pay.'

'Glad to hear it. Oh, and I'll need the afternoon off on Tuesday for my friend's mother's funeral, OK?'

Jeff gritted his teeth and nodded. 'Fine.'

'Well, then, I'd better get back to work. Chris will be wondering where I am.'

Then she stood, smoothed down her cargo pants and T-shirt, shook his hand, then left the room with as much stature as if she were wearing Chanel couture, not merely the only clean clothes she had managed to find at home.

The next few days went by in a blur.

Cara had to prepare Chris for the big day as well as wanting to be on the phone to Gracie as much as she could be. And Adam had disappeared. Cara had no idea if he was even staying at the hotel any longer. She should have been frantic, she was so busy, but her mind was only half on the job. She had all the distance she had so recently craved and it made her feel worse than ever.

She missed his company, his face, even his argumenta- tiveness terribly. But how could she have been surprised? He had obviously run for the hills the first chance he had. And why not? A guy like him didn't need to be caught up in the small-time problems of a suburban girl like her. He had gone above and beyond for her and for Gracie. And for that she would love him for ever.

Tuesday afternoon, Cara left the hotel once more to join

Gracie at her mother's funeral. And she was amazed to find that Gracie, the flippant airhead of the crew, had become a grown-up overnight. Her stepfather was inconsolable, and her half-sister and half-brother, who were so much younger than she, were a mess. But Gracie held it all together beautifully. Cara was amazed at her friend's fortitude.

She half hoped Adam would be there. But he never showed. Though he did send the most beautiful spray of gardenias, Gracie's favourite flowers. How he had ever known that, Cara had no idea. Even though she was finding herself becoming more and more desperate to know where he was and what he was doing, the flowers represented a small ray of hope.

Afterwards, Maya Rampling, the editor of *Fresh* magazine, insisted Cara accompany her in her town car back to Gracie's stepfather's house for the wake.

'So how is the big gig going?' Maya asked. 'Is television everything you imagined it would be?'

'Everything and more,' Cara joked.

'So what's Chris Geyer like?'

'Who?'

'Come on, Cara,' Maya said, a thin silver eyebrow rising in disappointment, 'Jeff Whatsit from the TV station has already been in touch in a mad panic to make sure I realise the fact that I know every detail means I will not say a thing now, but can have the exclusive in two weeks. He's like a terrier. Ferocious yet kind of cuddly all the same. I like him.'

'Despite everything, I kinda do too.'

'From what I hear, young Chris took quite a shine to you as well. Did you outshine the other lasses in his eyes?'

'Oh, no. At least one of them has outshone the lot of us.'

Maya sighed. 'So true love reigns in the end.'

Cara bit her lip and nodded. 'I guess it does.'

'So you haven't been having a mad fling with a grip? I always liked the sound of that job title: Grip.'

'No,' Cara laughed. 'I didn't have a mad fling with a grip.'

Maya flicked a telling glance Cara's way and she fought to smile calmly back.

'Don't mess with me, darling, I'm too old and too frosty to sit here and pretend to believe your hogwash. If a grip didn't steal your heart, somebody did. You're all pale and sickly and it's not just young Gracie's loss that has made you look this way.'

Cara chose her words carefully. 'You have to admit, my being in that atmosphere for the last couple of weeks can't have helped the situation any. The whole set-up has been put in place to create the perfect location in which two people could fall in love.'

'Bah! People fall in love in factories, in diners, on tops of mountains. Location is a small part of the story, what matters is the people. So, tell me, my sweet, *did somebody steal your heart*?'

Cara shrugged, but not with much effort. Her whole body felt bruised, way more than after she had hurt herself during the baseball game. They were just superficial injuries. For some reason her whole body ached. Maybe she was getting the flu.

'Maybe a little,' she admitted. 'But it doesn't matter. I was there to work and you know me. It's always about the job. Not about me.'

'Well, it's damn well about time it is about you, Cara. You don't always have to play the good girl. You're all grown up now; you've been away from the familial home for nearly ten years. It's time you gave yourself a break.'

'I don't think I have it in me to play the bad girl, Maya.'

'Don't be bad, be true. True to yourself. Not to some

perfect vision of yourself. Listen to your heart and do as it tells you. It pumps your lifeblood through every inch of your body, so it certainly should be given a lot more credit than you have given it to date.'

Cara had nothing to say to that. She stared out the window, watching the trees swaying with the hot, humid wind that had been buffeting the city all the day, signifying a change was in the air.

That night Cara took her time smoothing down Chris's tie as he readied himself for the final day of the shoot. She wanted to savour every moment of this, her last day.

'Are you ready, buddy?' Cara asked him for the final time.

'More than I ever thought I would be,' Chris said, his voice steady. He turned to her and grasped her hands in both of his. 'And a great deal of that is thanks to you. Without your support I could very well have been turned to the dark side by my solemn friend.'

Cara noted he did not use Adam's name. And she knew that Chris knew exactly what she was going through, a slow, sure but necessary breaking of her heart. Cara braved a smile and clasped a tight hold of his hand, amazed that she had found herself such a firm friend under such unusual circumstances.

'Did you think you would find what you were looking for from this process?'

Chris thought about it a moment. 'I did. But in the end I found more than I ever imagined I would.'

'You really love her, don't you, Chris?'

'I really do.'

Cara threw herself into Chris's arms and gave him a huge bear hug. 'I can tell. You're glowing.'

'That's what the power of love will do to a guy.'

Cara nodded. 'It suits you.'

Chris held her at arm's length, his eyes narrowing as he took her in. 'Along the same lines, what's with all the sunken eyes and stooping walk? You look like the world is on your shoulders.'

Cara moved away and headed over to the clothes rack, and began flicking blindly through the suits and shirts. 'I think I'm getting the flu. Or something. I've got the whole aching-muscle-sleepless-night thing going on.'

'I guess that's what the power of love can do to a girl.'

Cara pretended she hadn't heard him. She picked out a tie and held it up to him. 'Do you think this would be a better choice?'

Chris held a hand over hers, and her panicky gaze flickered to him.

'You should tell him.'

She opened her mouth to ask who but thought better of it. Instead she gave him a weak shrug. 'Can't.'

Chris let forth an expletive that she hadn't imagined such a sweet guy would have in his repertoire. 'The two of you are as bad as one another. And here I am, having the most exciting time of my life, yet at the same time caught in the middle, watching the two of you pine away for one another.'

'I'm not pining,' Cara insisted. But her mind was off and running in a whole other direction. *He's pining? Wherever the guy is, he's actually pining?*

But Chris glared back at her.

'Sorry,' she said. 'I was supposed to be the one giving you a pep talk.'

'I don't need a pep talk. I know what I want and I am going out there to get it. Can you say the same for yourself?'

She couldn't give him a straight answer so, borrowing a

move from someone she knew, she just shrugged and let him fill the silence.

'Just don't take too long to figure it out, Cara.'

And then, without a doubt in the world, Chris walked out of the room, more than ready to propose to the woman he loved.

But he was stopped the moment he hit the hallway by Adam on the fly. Chris held up a hand to fend off his friend and just kept on walking. 'Where the hell have you been these last couple of days?'

'Working. Wheeling. Dealing.'

'Pfft,' Chris scoffed. 'Hiding, more like it. And whatever you have to say can keep until after the filming.'

Adam settled into a slow walk a few feet behind his friend. Wow. He had never seen Chris so determined. He walked with a purpose. His usually fuzzy edges were clear and crisp. He even looked taller than usual. Adam told him so.

Chris wasn't in the mood. 'I said don't.'

'But it's true.'

Chris stopped only to press the button on the lift and Adam was able to catch up.

'I only came up here to wish you good luck today.'

Adam flinched under his friend's silent wary gaze.

'I mean it, Chris.' Adam placed a hand on Chris's shoulder. 'I can see how much this experience has changed you. Helped you. Made you happy. And for that there is no way I can make any sort of complaint.'

'Are you joshing me?'

'No, I'm not. I am here to shake your hand and to wish you all the best. Treat her well and I'll leave it up to you to make sure she does the same for you.'

Chris was still not completely convinced.

'I can't complain that you are a total romantic, mate,'

Adam said. 'You need to be at least a little fanciful to be a really good inventor. And you're the best I've ever seen.'

Adam held out a hand in conciliation but Chris would have none of that. He grabbed the hand only to pull Adam into a hearty bear hug.

'Thanks, mate. That means the world to me.'

Adam gave Chris's back one last slap before pulling away.

'I could offer you some pretty similar advice right now, Adam,' Chris said with a sympathetic smile playing about his mouth.

Adam blinked.

'Please,' Chris said. 'You can try to pull the strong, silent method on me but it will never work. I've known you too long. But you have shown me today you can stay out of my business when it is warranted so I will show you the same courtesy.'

The lift binged and the doors slid open.

'Saved by the bell,' Chris said, stepping into the lift.

'Now go get her, mate,' Adam said, acting the jovial friend again. 'Make sure one of those kisses she gets is from me. And tell her so.'

Chris nodded. And as the doors closed Adam could sense his friend leaving him as his thoughts reached out to someone else. A woman waiting for him to reveal himself to her. Adam only hoped that woman knew how good she was about to have it.

He looked back down the hallway and saw Chris's closed suite door. He knew Cara would be behind that door. Alone. And after having sat with Chris all evening she must have been thinking along much the same lines that he was.

They had been thrown together under such odd circumstances and neither had any idea if what they felt would survive in the real world. So he had left. He had gone home. And it had killed him not seeing her.

He could only wait and see and hope that she had felt the same way.

CHAPTER TWELVE

CARA watched in rapt amazement as Chris and Maggie declared their love for one another on the balcony where they had first met. If the rest of the shoot had felt like some sort of hyper-reality, this felt like a fairy tale, pure and simple. The candles, the star-spangled night sky, the trailing ivy, it was more beautiful than anything she had ever seen. How could a girl refuse a proposal in such surroundings?

But she knew that Maggie would not have refused Chris's hand if they had been sitting across from one another in some dingy milk bar instead.

Cara wiped away a tear. While she felt so excited for Chris, her own heart was breaking. This was what she was giving up. But if she did as Chris suggested and told Adam how she felt, she would only be setting herself up for ever worse heartache. Adam had it in him to feel as strongly as Chris did, she knew that without a doubt. But she was not sure that he was ready to admit it.

She sniffed back her sadness and concentrated on the scene in front of her. Chris was about to drop the second part of his bombshell and she could not wait to see how Maggie would react. Would she jump for joy, would she faint, or would the news hit her as it did Cara and make her want to run for her life?

Chris took a deep breath and squeezed Maggie's hands. A small shy smile flitted across his face. 'Oh, and by the way,' he said, 'I am a billionaire.'

The whole crew held its collective breath.

Maggie's response could not have been more unexpected. With a big grin, she slapped Chris on the arm and said, 'Well, good for you!'

As Chris wrapped Maggie up in a delighted embrace the whole crew burst into spontaneous laughter and applause.

Cara stared at the couple in shock. What a response. *Good for him. He's rich. Now let's get on with things.*

The simplicity of it all hit her like a kick to the stomach. Her heart rate struck up a solid rhythm as she suddenly realised what she had to do.

Adam leant against the doorway, his chosen spot affording a view through the cameras and assorted equipment to his friend who stood on the balcony of the Ivy Hotel.

But more importantly, it afforded him an unimpeded view of Cara. She stood by the central camera, ready to be a rock of support to Chris in this, the most important moment of his life.

She was dressed down in jeans and T-shirt, obviously making sure she was not about to outshine the woman of the moment, the delightfully unshockable Maggie.

As the sweet blonde girl was released from Chris's embrace, she stumbled. Chris reached out to catch her, and the two of them faced each other with matching blushes. Adam's heart jerked in his chest. Damn it! He even felt something akin to tears burning the backs of his eyes.

Maggie whispered something that had Chris and the crew laughing. Adam moved away from his hiding spot and quietly eased closer to the action. He slowly walked around the outside of the room until he found a spot at the far right of the cameras. He was still in the shadows, but from there he could see Cara's face. Her hands were covering her mouth and she had tears pouring down her face.

With her heart on her sleeve she looked more beautiful

to him than she ever had before. Adam wanted to go to her, and hug her and kiss the tears from her cheeks.

Who was he kidding? He wanted to do more than that. He wasn't looking for a date for Saturday night, he wasn't looking for a month-long fling. He wanted to wake up looking into those bright green eyes, he wanted to kiss those beautiful lips, and he wanted to caress those soft curls every day for the rest of his life. He wanted to introduce her to his father, for heaven's sake!

He finally realised that all the signs led to one thing. He was head over heels in love.

At that moment, the rain that had been threatening to wash down on the city all day finally hit. It rained with such unceasing force it would have drowned out the couple's voices if it had come but a minute earlier.

Everyone on the balcony sprinted inside the ballroom. Jeff grabbed every spare guy to help shut the balcony doors to shield their precious equipment from the rain buffeting the outside of the hotel.

Cara went straight to Chris and Maggie, making sure they were OK. She all but hugged the life out of each of them.

Then once the rain was no more than a steady hum against the windows, Jeff called out, 'And that's a wrap! See you all at the wrap party at Lunar on Friday night!'

The crew exploded into raucous cheers, hugging and clapping and generally whooping it up. Then as quickly as they started, they stopped, and with happy chatter they began to pack up the equipment. Before Adam had time to catch his breath, one by one they began to leave. Almost immediately the room started to clear. He watched as Cara gave everyone a hug, saying goodbye. It was over. It was all over.

They were leaving. Cara was leaving. And if he wanted

to do those things with her for the rest of his life, it would be up to him to tell her so. Adam remembered back to the Saturday Night Cocktails dinner where Kelly had professed that was exactly what she needed.

'Cara. Stay.' The words wrenched from him with such power the whole set went quiet. The grips slowly lowered their bags; the sound guys stopped their unplugging; Adam felt every eye swing his way, but there was only one set of eyes he cared about. A pair of glittering cat's eyes that belonged to the woman who had long since awoken his dormant heart.

Cara turned, her expression puzzled. 'Adam?'

She had every right to be confused. He had avoided her for days. But since he no longer had an ounce of confusion remaining in his body he got on with what he had to do.

'I said, stay.'

She blinked and it took all of his strength not to run to her and drag her into his arms and kiss that gorgeous puzzled look from her face. Instead he sent her his most encouraging grin, lifted a finger, and beckoned her to him.

What the hell does he think he's doing?

Cara looked about her. The whole crew had stopped packing and were watching in smiling silence. Whatever Adam was up to, there was no way they were going to miss a minute of it.

Cara hastened to Adam's side.

'What do you think you are doing?' she asked through gritted teeth.

'Something I should have done a long time ago.'

Adam grabbed her hand and tugged her to him so fast her breath released on a shocked sigh. He tipped her back and planted a long, hard kiss upon her mouth. Over the sound of angels singing in her ears Cara heard whooping and catcalls of two dozen crew members.

Finally, when Adam deigned to release her from his liquefying embrace, Cara pulled away and brought a shaking hand to her mouth.

'Cara,' Adam said. 'I'm asking you to stay. With me. I'm asking you to be mine.'

She had barely recovered from his delicious kiss, and any words he had to say came to her as outright gibberish. Surely he couldn't have said he was asking her to be his?

'But why?' she asked.

He offered her a lopsided smile that had her smiling right back. 'Are you really telling me that you haven't seen the signs?' he asked. 'For a guy who is a professed bachelor, have you not seen that I have had eyes for no one but you since the moment you walked into my life on your sexy red shoes?'

Cara swallowed, unsure, uncertain, desperate for him to tell her what she needed to hear. Then he smiled at her and her knees turned to jelly and she was glad she was wrapped tight in his arms. He shifted his grip so that she was moulded so perfectly against him she could barely breathe. His words then came to her, low and alluring, and soft enough for only her to hear.

'Hmm. Not a good enough reason? How about because no two people ever tried so hard to deny what was best for them? And only if the both of us take the leap can we ever see if what we feel is real.'

Somebody gave a great big sniff and Cara came back down to earth with a thud. The two dozen others in the room came back into sharp focus.

'Why couldn't you be the one with the fear of public speaking?' she asked through gritted teeth.

Adam turned to the crew and said, 'Would you guys mind giving us a minute?'

'Change of plans!' Jeff called out instantaneously. 'Wrap party is in my room, right now!'

The crew hustled as though a whip were cracking at their backs. Chris and Maggie blew the pair of them a big kiss before heading out a hidden side door together.

When Adam and Cara were alone, with nothing more than the sound of steady rain on the balcony as a companion, Cara asked, 'Do you know what you are asking?'

'Mmm hmm,' he whispered against her ear.

'But are you sure you're ready for this? Ready for me?'

'More than ready.'

'And what do you think this is exactly?' His breath against her neck was making her giddy.

'I don't know if I can put it into words,'

'Mr Tyler, I thought your special gift was words.'

'It is. This is bigger than words. But whatever this is, I don't ever want it to go away. So what do you say, Ms Marlowe?' Adam said, burying his face beneath the hair curling at her neck, his hot breath sending pulsating shivers down her back. 'Do you promise to be mine for as long as we can stand each other?'

Cara suddenly could not have cared if they were standing in the middle of the Melbourne Cricket Ground with a packed stadium looking on. This moment was too important to worry about such trivial details as location.

Now was the time to swallow her own fear and be true. She felt a calm come over her as she said, 'I promise to be yours for ever.'

Adam stopped nuzzling. 'Say that again,' he demanded softly.

He waited until she lowered her gaze and looked directly into his eyes. He held his breath and had no desire to take another until he had heard those words again.

'Adam,' she said with a vulnerable shrug, 'I am hopelessly in love with you. And if you will have me, I promise to be yours for ever.'

He hadn't been able to put the feeling into words, but she, ever the strong one, had. She deserved as good as she gave. He took her face in his hands and said what had to be said.

'Cara, sweetheart, there is nothing hopeless about a love that is returned to you tenfold.' He swept her into his arms once more, bruising her lips with as much passion as he could give.

'But I want you to know I want nothing from you,' she said when she next had the chance.

'Tough. You take me, you get everything I have to give.'

'Adam, no.'

'OK, then. So long as you promise not to give me anything of yours either.' He had her just where he wanted her. With a rising smile he added, 'I will never want your strange little apartment block. You can keep *it* for ever.'

Cara slapped him on the chest. 'You rotter! St Kilda Storeys is a fantastic piece of real estate, I'll have you know. It's worth twenty-five per cent more now than the day I bought it.'

Adam grabbed Cara by the hand to stop her struggling. 'I don't care what it's worth. But I want you to know *I* know how much the place means to you. How much your independence means to you. So, though I am never going to let you out of my arms for another minute, I want you to keep your building,' he reiterated. 'For you alone. As a safety net.'

She believed him. He saw it in her eyes. He felt it in her touch as she melted against him. Then just as suddenly she threw herself wholly into his arms and Adam rocked back at the force.

'Whoa, sweetheart,' Adam said. 'What's that for?'

'It's for being an amazing man.'

She pulled away and looked into his eyes, the love she felt for him hitting him in waves, and it was all he could do not to wrench her back and kiss her for all she meant to him.

'Adam, don't you understand?' she said. 'You have no choice. What's mine is yours. You get me, you get too many clothes in your closet, you get Kelly and Gracie on our doorstep at least once a week, and you get my old place.'

He screwed up his nose. 'And what am I meant to do with it?'

She slapped him on the arm. 'Don't you screw your nose up at my beautiful building. Or I'll make you live in it.'

Adam made to pull away, his feet shuffling on the spot as though if she let him go he would bolt for the hills like the Road Runner. It made her laugh and that sweet tinkling sound was the final straw.

He stopped pulling, he stopped shuffling, and he wrapped his arms so far around her he was almost hugging himself.

'So we'll live in your cosy little building, then.'

Her beautiful eyes narrowed. 'Are you serious?'

He shrugged. 'Wherever you are, I am. Whether it be in my nice, new, air-conditioned home with its guest rooms, its salt-water pool, its billiard room, its acres of tended gardens, or in your St Kilda Storeys apartment where Gracie will pop in every morning with her news of the previous night's marriage proposal.'

Cara bit at her lip and he knew he almost had her.

'So there we'll stay,' Adam continued. 'No sleeping in…together. Scenic views of the next-door neighbour's garage wall. A spare couch for Kelly and Simon to sleep on after a late night DVD jag—'

'OK, stop!' she finally acquiesced. 'Stop. You've made your point.'

She hugged him tight back and he couldn't believe how wonderful he felt.

'And a good point it is,' she said. 'I will move in with you instead?' He could hear the uncertainty in her voice so he kissed her sweet nose.

'Sweetheart, you are coming home with me as of today if I have to carry you over my shoulder kicking and screaming to get you there.'

She grinned back at him with such force he knew he had her.

'And so what will we do with St Kilda Storeys?' he asked.

Still wrapped tight in his arms she looked up at him. 'I think we'll keep it for ever and ever. It has served beautifully as a place for young strays and I wouldn't want to take that opportunity away from the next generation. If I sold it they'd probably tear it down and build gleaming new condos. Nope. St Kilda Storeys stays.'

'Fine.'

'Besides, where else would Gracie go?'

A month later, Cara went back to her bottom-floor apartment of St Kilda Storeys to spend one last night. And she went with a bang.

Kelly and Simon came over bearing a cask of sparkling apple juice. Chris and his fiancée Maggie joined them, neither of them remembering to bring the bags of crisps that had been sitting on their kitchen bench. Gracie arrived late, but had managed to pick up an industrial-sized box of Belgian chocolates from a visiting gentleman who had given them to all the cute young croupiers in the high rollers room as a tip.

While Kelly set up the room with borrowed cushions from Gracie's couch upstairs and beanbags from another neighbour, Simon moved the television from Cara's old bedroom into the lounge, and Adam made caramel popcorn.

'Wow,' Cara whispered in Adam's ear as he piled the snack into a big bowl. 'The man can cook. I am impressed.'

'Dad's third wife. She lived on the stuff.'

'And you said they gave you nothing. Caramel popcorn is not nothing.'

Adam caught her around the waist, pulling her to him and placing a kiss upon her nose. 'My little eternal optimist. You are too good for me.'

'Not too good. Just about perfect.'

'Come on, guys!' Kelly yelled from her seat in the lounge. 'It's starting!'

Cara grabbed the first full bowl and took it into the lounge where she was greeted with a mass of flailing arms reaching for the popcorn.

'Turn it up,' someone demanded and Gracie did the honours.

Then as the first episode of *The Billionaire Bachelor* lit the screen a barrage of popcorn hit the television.

'Hey,' Cara called out, 'I just had the carpet professionally cleaned.' But the popcorn merely flew thicker and faster.

'Look, there's Maggie.' Chris shifted so quickly in his beanbag Maggie all but rolled off his lap.

'Wait up, cowboy, I'm right here too, you know,' Maggie said, her bright blue eyes glinting.

Chris's ears burned red. 'So you are.' Then he gave her a light, lingering kiss on the mouth.

Cara sighed as she watched them. Two young people in love. Two young people who had found each other under the most trying, unusual circumstances, and it was obvious to all how right they were for each other.

As though picking up on the romance in the air, Kelly and Simon snuggled closer on the couch, Simon's hand reaching out to rest on Kelly's tummy as she laid her head on his shoulder.

Cara's gaze was immediately drawn to Adam, his bulk taking up so much of the small kitchen. He was leaning back against the kitchen counter, and his arms were crossed, but the latent frustration that had blazed from him since the day they had met was gone. His relaxed pose was all real as he watched the gang with a smile on his face. It was a smile full of understanding and hope.

Then, as though sensing she was watching him, he blinked and turned his eyes her way. And his smile changed. Where it had been lit by hope, it was now lit by the fulfilment of that hope. She knew, as if he had whispered the words in her ear, that he owed it all to her. Cara's breath caught in her throat, the impact of his loving gaze was so great. So great but so beautiful.

With a slight flick of his head he beckoned her. And without argument she went to him, burying herself in his solid embrace, breathing deep of his glorious scent and feeling more than safe enveloped in his amazing warmth. After several long moments feeling as if she were floating on air, she heard the voices of her friends cut in.

'Come on, guys! Come join us!'

Adam pulled away from the kitchen bench and, with his arms still wrapped about her, led Cara to the leather couch. Simon and Kelly shuffled up. And Cara tucked her feet beneath her as she snuggled against Adam on the couch.

Gracie shot them a big grin from her spot lying on the cushions on the floor.

'So I'm taking bets,' Gracie said as the show went to its

first ad break, half of which was taken up with Revolution Wireless's new campaign. 'Who do you reckon our bachelor is going to choose? And how long until they break up?'

The popcorn that had been flying thick and fast at the television earlier now came pelting Gracie's way along with a barrage of not-nice words. She squealed and covered her face with her arms.

'Hey, no fair. Don't pick on the single girl. I'm trying very hard not to be sick, there is so much schmaltz in the air right now. So I think I deserve a little leeway for bitterness.'

'It's your turn next, Gracie,' Maggie predicted.

'What about Dean?' Kelly asked. 'He thought you were a bit of all right.'

'So where is he now?' Gracie demanded.

'Yeah,' Chris said, 'where is Dean? I thought he was coming too.'

'Working,' Adam said. 'Always working.'

Gracie shrugged. 'Well, there you go. I'm a player and he's a worker. It's just wouldn't work. Seems you guys are stuck with me. Just keep an extra set of clean linen in the house in case I need some company and I'll be a happy girl for ever.'

Cara grinned. Simply enjoying the moment. Her friends all together, all smiling and happy, all helping her give her old home a grand send-off. The man she loved keeping her wrapped safe in her arms.

She was one of a bunch of decision-makers in the house and she didn't care a lick. She was happy to sit back and let someone else make the decisions right now. She would just go with the flow. If she had to give up the remote control in order to have this abundance of hope, and love, and excitement for the future, then so be it.

Adam could have the remote control, as he had her heart. And as far as she was concerned he could do with them as he pleased.

Cara clinked against her glass with beautifully manicured fingernails. 'I would like to make a toast.'

The gang noisily fought over mismatched cups and glasses until they were all ready.

'To Cary Grant,' Cara said, shooting Adam a glance full of meaning.

'To Cary Grant,' the rest of the gang mimicked cheerfully before gulping down their apple juice.

Adam's eyes softened and she leant in and kissed him, not caring who in the world was there to see it.

'Who's Cary Grant?' Maggie asked in a loud whisper and received a barrage of cushions thrown at her face.

'You really are a hick, aren't you?' Chris asked, and received a cushion wallop across the face for his efforts.

'Wait. It's back on!' he shouted, his face lighting up in amazement and blushing furiously at the same time as he watched himself on television.

The others settled into their positions and Cara snuck out of her seat. She beckoned to Adam, who came to her all too readily.

'What is it?' he whispered as she took him by the hand and led him out the front door and into the communal hallway at the front of the building. He kept looking over his shoulder back towards the gang inside. 'We're going to miss it.'

'We were there, doofus. I can even tell you how it ends if you're that worked up about it.'

On the word 'doofus' she had him hooked. He grabbed her around the waist and walked her backwards out the door and into the open air.

'Doofus? Is that any way to talk to the man you love?'

'Who says you're the man I love?'

'You do. And often. And if you keep pretending it's not true, I'm just going to have to torture you.'

He trudged down the big cement front steps and she had to stand on his feet so as not to lose her balance.

'OK. Stop! I give up. If you go any further I am going to fall.'

'I won't let you.'

Cara stopped her complaining and looked into his gorgeous blue eyes. Of course he wouldn't let her fall. She'd fallen only once in their relationship and she intended staying that way, especially since he had caught her in his strong arms.

'Now you've got me out here,' Adam said, his eyes dancing, 'what are you going to do with me?'

Cara grinned and stood high on her toes so she could kiss him. She could feel the smile on his lips as he kissed her back. And it wasn't the kiss of a passion they were afraid might extinguish if they did not drink of it desperately. It was a kiss that held the remembrance of many kisses gone, and the knowledge there would be many more kisses to come. It was a kiss that matched the steady heat and delicious languor of the long, hot summer that stretched out before them. It was a kiss that held all the time in the world.

Locals in shorts and T-shirts trailed the path in front of the old red St Kilda Storeys building and off to the beach, to nightclubs and to local restaurants. But Cara and Adam were exactly where they wanted to be.

The location was entirely irrelevant, so long as they were together.

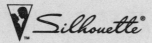

Silhouette®

ROMANTIC SUSPENSE

**Excitement, danger and
passion guaranteed**

INTIMATE MOMENTS™

In February 2007
Silhouette Intimate Moments®
will become
Silhouette® Romantic Suspense.

Look for it wherever you buy books!

Visit Silhouette Books at www.eHarlequin.com   SIMRSI 106

REQUEST YOUR FREE BOOKS!

2 FREE NOVELS PLUS 2 FREE GIFTS!

SILHOUETTE *Romance*®

From Today to Forever...

YES! Please send me 2 FREE Silhouette Romance® novels and my 2 FREE gifts. After receiving them, if I don't wish to receive any more books, I can return the shipping statement marked "cancel." If I don't cancel, I will receive 4 brand-new novels every month and be billed just $3.57 per book in the U.S., or $4.05 per book in Canada, plus 25¢ shipping and handling per book and applicable taxes, if any*. That's a savings of over 15% off the cover price! I understand that accepting the 2 free books and gifts places me under no obligation to buy anything. I can always return a shipment and cancel at any time. Even if I never buy another book from Silhouette, the two free books and gifts are mine to keep forever.

210 SDN EEWU   310 SDN EEW6

Name _____ (PLEASE PRINT)

Address _____ Apt. _____

City _____ State/Prov. _____ Zip/Postal Code _____

Signature (if under 18, a parent or guardian must sign)

Mail to Silhouette Reader Service™:

IN U.S.A.
P.O. Box 1867
Buffalo, NY
14240-1867

IN CANADA
P.O. Box 609
Fort Erie, Ontario
L2A 5X3

Not valid to current Silhouette Romance subscribers.

Want to try two free books from another line?
Call 1-800-873-8635 or visit www.morefreebooks.com.

* Terms and prices subject to change without notice. NY residents add applicable sales tax. Canadian residents will be charged applicable provincial taxes and GST. This offer is limited to one order per household. All orders subject to approval. Credit or debit balances in a customer's account(s) may be offset by any other outstanding balance owed by or to the customer. Please allow 4 to 6 weeks for delivery.

SROM06

COMING NEXT MONTH

#1842 A VOW TO KEEP—Cara Colter
Rick Chase found himself promising to step back temporarily
into his old friend Linda Starr's life to help her out. But then he
met the woman she'd become—a woman with spirit, passion and
unmatched beauty! Promises could be troublesome. They demanded
more than he wanted to give, but had the potential to reward him
with more than he'd ever imagined!

#1843 BLIND-DATE MARRIAGE—Fiona Harper
Serena loves everything in life, except for blind dates! She's turned
her back on her unconventional upbringing, and her deepest wish is
to find the man to spend the rest of her life with…. Jake is a highly
successful and focused businessman. He's worked hard to escape
his roots, and now lives by one rule: *never* get married!

#1844 MILLIONAIRE DAD: WIFE NEEDED—
Natasha Oakley
Nick Regan-Phillips is a millionaire, and the world assumes he has
it all. But he's got a secret. He's a single dad, his daughter, Rosie, is
deaf and he's struggling to communicate with her. Lydia Stanford
is a beautiful award-winning journalist—and seemingly the only
person who can help Nick forge a bond with his daughter.

#1845 A MOTHER FOR HIS DAUGHTER—Ally Blake
How To Marry a Billionaire
Just as Gracie had run out of money and was about to book her
flight home to Australia she'd been rescued! A gorgeous Italian had
hired her to live in his magnificent Tuscan home and be nanny to
his little girl! Luca was thrilled—the new nanny had brought smiles
and laughter back into his daughter's life. He wanted Gracie to stay
forever—as his wife.…